# A BABY FOR THE ALPHA

## BAD ALPHA DADS
### Marissa Farrar

# A Baby for the Alpha: Bad Alpha Dads

Marissa Farrar

Published by Warwick House Press, 2018.

This is a work of fiction. Similarities to real people, places, or events are entirely coincidental.

A BABY FOR THE ALPHA: BAD ALPHA DADS

**First edition. January 30, 2018.**

Copyright © 2018 Marissa Farrar.

ISBN: 978-1386725664

Written by Marissa Farrar.

Bestselling and Award Winning Paranormal Romance authors are bringing you the baddest of the bad ALPHA dads. Keyword bad. So sexy, you'll want to teach them to be good. These shifter dads need all the help they can get, and we want to give it to them. Check out our website www.BadAlphaDads.com[2] for the release schedule and more about our fabulous authors.

---

# Chapter One

SHE RAN THROUGH THE forest, her breath heaving in and out of her lungs. Above her head, the moon hung low. Its white glow peeped through the spindly branches of the trees, never quite coming into full view, as though, like her, it didn't want to be seen. Night was her cover, but she didn't know how much use it would be. Her kind was as comfortable during the night as they were in the day.

Clutching all her worldly goods in a bag, which she held against her body, she moved as fast as she could. The baby inside her was bigger now, pushing up her internal organs, taking up the space where her lungs should be. This made it harder for her to breathe, but physical issues weren't the only reason for her shortness of breath. Fear clutched at her heart, and, as she ran, she turned to glance over her shoulder, certain he would be pursuing her.

He would kill her when he found out she had gone, but she had no choice. Her body was changing now, her bump too big to be able to hide much longer. She'd been lucky in that the baby had been positioned closer to her back, making her growing belly less noticeable, but soon it would be impossible for him not to notice, and when that happened, she knew it would be all over.

When it had just been her, she'd been able to put up with how things were, but now everything was different. As the pregnancy progressed, and she'd experienced the wonder of feeling the movements of her baby inside her, she'd known she wouldn't be able to let her child live through the life she'd been forced into. So she'd done the only thing she could.

She ran.

How many miles lay ahead? She had no way of knowing. All she focused on was putting as many between her and the place she had once thought of as home. Though on foot right now, because, despite her pregnancy, it was the safest, most reliable way for her to move, she knew she wouldn't be able to keep it up forever. The baby drained her energy, and soon enough she would need to find transport other than her own legs.

She could try to hide among the humans, but a shifter's gestation period was far shorter than a human's. If she needed to seek medical attention, or if the baby needed to be born in the hospital, what she was would be noticed immediately. Humans knew of the existence of supernaturals, but it wasn't them figuring out what she was that worried her so much. No, the reason for her concerns were that it was unusual for a shifter to give birth among humans, and that news would travel, no matter what distance she'd put between herself and the place she'd once thought of as home. And when that news did travel, it would eventually reach *his* ears, and, when it did, he would find her.

And then he would kill them both.

# Chapter Two

"I'M SORRY, CARTER. This just isn't working. We've tried. You know we have. I can't waste my life like this."

Alpha of Silver Creek Pack, Carter Reed, put out a hand to try to placate her. "Just one more cycle. Please. You never know."

Kimberly exhaled a deep sigh. "I'm not getting any younger, and neither are you, for that matter. You're almost thirty years old, and if this was going to happen, it would have by now."

"We don't know that." He hated the pleading tone in his voice—he wasn't a man who begged—but he couldn't help it. Desperation was starting to set in. As her alpha, he could have commanded her to stay, but he'd never had to force a woman into staying with him, and he wasn't about to start now. "These things take time."

She shook her head. "Not for an alpha male and alpha female, they don't. This obviously isn't right. I'm sorry. I can't give this any more of my time."

Carter watched as she turned from him, her tiny waist flaring into wide hips—child-bearing hips, he'd thought when he'd first seen her—and she sashayed away without even a backward glance, her shiny dark hair swinging down her slender back.

He grabbed the edge of his front door and slammed it shut with a bang that rattled through the rest of the house. He balled his fist and punched the wood. "Goddamn it!"

His anger wasn't heartbreak. He'd enjoyed the time he'd spent with Kimberly, but they'd both known why they were together. It was a mutual, unspoken agreement—with her wanting something from him, the opportunity to be alpha female, and him needing the one thing that would secure his place as pack leader. That wasn't saying he wouldn't miss her. She'd been filthy in bed, and he'd enjoyed having her willingly spread her legs for him at any moment. But as the months went by, and there had still been no sign of anything happening, they'd both started to get frustrated. Sex had never quite become a chore, but it was certainly heading in that direction, and he knew she'd been able to sense it, too. They'd been sniping at each other about ridiculous things, and the passionate sex had turned into angry sex. Not that he was complaining too much, but they'd both known it wasn't working.

*Shit.*

Kimberly had been the latest in a line of failed relationships. Hell, they could hardly be called relationships. They were arrangements. Agreements. He hadn't found his mate yet. In fact, he was starting to think such a thing didn't even exist. Everyone talked about a mythical mate, a bonding, but he thought it was as likely as love at first sight. You didn't need to find a bonded mate in order to have pups. His mother and father had been an arranged bonding, and they'd produced him just fine.

Before Kimberly had been Sara, and before Sara was Lizbeth. There had been at least a few before Lizbeth, but both their names and faces were starting to blend together now. With each arrangement, he'd done his best to get the female pregnant, but nothing had worked. His first mating, Allison, had left him because of it when he was twenty-three. They'd tried for two years to get her pregnant, doing ridiculous things before and after sex to try to get something to stick—him keeping his balls at a certain temperature, which wasn't easy as a hot-blooded shifter, and her lying with her legs up in the air. Nothing had worked, and in the end Allison had announced she wasn't wasting her life in this way, and had mated with another wolf in his pack. That had hurt. He'd actually cared about that girl.

Now, six years later, he was running out of nubile young women in the pack. He could have any of them for the taking—he only had to say the word—but he'd known some of the girls only just turning eighteen since they were small pups, and he couldn't bring himself to think of them in that way.

He'd never liked the idea of a single mate for the rest of his life, anyway. Who the hell would want that? It would be like spending every day surrounded by the most sumptuous buffet, but being told you could only eat one item on the table every day forever. It didn't matter how much he liked the one dish, he was going to get sick of it eventually and start longing for all the other delicious things on offer.

But his time was running out. He needed to provide a child—male or female, didn't matter—to continue his family's hold on the position of alpha. He could sense other males in the pack already sniffing around, knowing the chance to challenge his place was coming up soon. What the fuck was wrong with him?

Carter couldn't stand to spend the rest of the day holed up inside the walls of his home. He'd smash the place apart before the end of the day. He wasn't someone who coped with emotions well, preferring a physical outlet to anything that was troubling him. A run through the forest in wolf form would soon put any worries out of his head. Problem was, even after the run, he still had to come home and face things. The pack would hear of Kimberly leaving soon enough, and then he was going to have some questions to answer. The pack couldn't continue with him at its head if he was unable to provide them with an heir to take on his role of alpha or female alpha when the pup came of age.

No, he preferred to be as wolf when he was feeling like this. Hell, he preferred to be as wolf, full stop. Life was easier as a beast. Fighting, fucking, feeding. That was all it came down to when he was in animal form. At times, he could see the appeal to becoming a lone wolf and living his life that way, not needing to worry about pack hierarchy and expectations. But the truth was, he loved his pack. Yes, it was frustrating at times, but his family had been alphas for generations now, and he wanted to remain as head of the pack. The thought of being forced to step down because of something that was completely out of his control filled him with shame. He was the biggest man and wolf in the entire pack, and he could fight off any of the other wolves sniffing around his position as alpha, but if they could get a female pregnant and produce the pack's next generation of alphas, and he couldn't... well, then, he'd have no choice but to willingly step down.

Carter left his house—the largest in town, and another thing he'd be forced to relinquish if he didn't produce the next generation of alpha—and crossed the compound. The house had always been a place filled with family. Cubs, aunts, uncles, and of course the alpha and alpha female, looking down on what they'd played such a huge part in creating. That was how he remembered his family, but fate hadn't been kind. He'd lost his mother when he was sixteen, and his father two years later, which was when he'd taken over as alpha.

The small town which housed the Silver Creek pack consisted of Main Street and a couple of blocks behind on both sides. It was barely a town, really, but there weren't enough pack members to make the place any larger. Other supernaturals, like the vampires, preferred to be alone, and tended to blend with the humans, but shifters were different. They liked to form communities of their own and stuck to their own kind. Outsiders weren't welcomed, and the idea of a human or vampire attempting to move into a place run by a pack was laughable.

Carter's motorcycle sat on the street outside. He didn't need to worry about a helmet or leathers. Not only did he have supernatural agility and senses, he also healed faster than humans, so if he were to come off, it was unlikely that he'd do himself any permanent damage. He swung his leg over the seat. It wouldn't take him long to get out of town, but he didn't want to walk. All he wanted to do was escape and put as much space between him and Kimberly as possible.

About to kick the bike into gear, someone jogged toward him, his hand lifted to catch Carter's attention. Carter groaned inwardly. This was exactly the thing he'd been hoping to avoid by getting out of town quickly. Perhaps he should have stayed in the house and locked the door instead.

Liam Goodman was only a couple of years younger than Carter. Good-looking, with a muscular frame and a natural charm, he was most likely going to be the one after Carter's position as alpha if things didn't work out.

"Hey, Carter. I just passed Kimberly. She said things hadn't worked out between you."

Carter scowled. "You're not sniffing around my leftovers again, are you, Liam?"

Liam laughed, and then threw Carter a wink. "How do you know I hadn't already been there first?"

Carter's fists tightened around the handles of his bike. "You know who you're speaking to? Don't be so fucking disrespectful of your alpha."

"Might not be for long, though, huh? Everyone is talking, Carter. It's not even like you can hand over to your beta. Everyone knows James wouldn't be cut out for the job."

It was true. James Salter wasn't alpha material. Carter had chosen him as beta because the other man was so different from him. James was a gentler soul, who was happily mated to his childhood sweetheart, Anna. He liked his books and handled the pack's finances, plus James never made any noises about wishing he was able to take the next step up in the pack. James was the brains, while Carter supplied the brawn.

Carter wished he had a younger brother, or hell, a cousin, even, so he'd have someone he could hand over the role of alpha to, and hope they'd do a better job at maintaining their family's bloodline, but he didn't. Carter was too proud a man to ever admit that he was lonely in his world. He was surrounded by other pack members, but they each had families of their own. He, of all wolves, should be confident in his place within the pack, but often he experienced a pang of envy toward the subordinate wolves, with their big families and content lives. At least he assumed they were content. It wasn't as though he'd ever taken the time to ask one of them.

He remembered Liam still standing there, smirking at him. Carter hated that the other shifter knew exactly what was going on in his personal life.

He roared the bike to life. "I've got places to be. Now, stop wasting my time."

Not giving the other shifter time to reply, he released the throttle and got the big bike moving. He glanced in the wing mirror and exhaled a breath as Liam grew smaller in the glass.

# Chapter Three

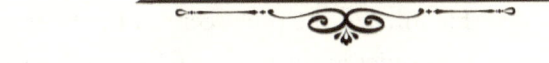

HE SHOULDN'T HAVE FELT better by leaving his pack behind, but he did.

Once he got out of town, Carter swerved the bike off the road and into the bordering forest. Instantly, he was able to breathe more easily. The bike bumped and jolted over rough terrain, and he slowed his speed and took the time to maneuver around fallen tree trunks and clumps of bushes. He wanted to get deep enough into the forest that he didn't have to worry about another of his pack noticing either his bike or his scent and following him out here. Most wolves liked to run as a group, but today he just wanted to be alone with his own thoughts. Or even better, not to have to think at all.

Carter stopped the bike and climbed off. He kicked down the stand. No one should come across the bike out here, not unless they were specifically looking for it. He reached up into the air, stretching out the muscles of his neck and shoulders. The tension from his fight with Kimberly had knotted everything up. He was a big man, bulked with muscle, and when he was stressed, he felt it in every inch of his body.

Already more relaxed, he reached to the bottom of his t-shirt and pulled it up over his head. He dropped the material onto the seat of the bike. His hands went to the button of the soft, worn jeans currently encasing his ass and thighs, and he

13

popped it open and unzipped the fly. Toeing off the boots he wore, he left them tumbled together. Finally, he shucked the jeans from his hips and kicked them away. He didn't need to worry about underwear; he never wore any.

Naked in the forest, he rolled his shoulders and planted his bare feet in the dirt. He inhaled the pine scent of the trees and listened as the birds grew quiet in the trees and insects departed the area. It was as though he gave off a type of radiation that allowed the other inhabitants to know something supernatural was around. Things were normal when he was in man form, and also as wolf, but when he was in that in-between point, just as he was on the brink of change, the rest of the forest grew quiet.

His wolf form was always right beneath the surface, waiting to be called upon.

As he threw himself forward, he shed the skin of his human form. By the time he hit the ground, his hands and feet were already paws. A bushy tail sprung out from his spine, and large ears folded from the top of his head.

Carter was as big a wolf as he was man. Thick, luxurious black fur covered his heavily muscled body, and he paused to shake it out before continuing on his run. Fallen leaves crunched beneath his paws, and the earthy scent of the forest floor filled his nostrils. His sense of smell was acute as a man, but in wolf form it became a hundred times stronger. All around him, small creatures darted away, worried they'd become a snack, but Carter wasn't interested in eating. All he wanted to do was run until he was so exhausted he could no longer think.

But as he ran, a different scent drifted over to him, stronger than the pine infused air. What was that? Something sweet, yet warming, like vanilla cupcakes recently taken out of the oven. His nostrils flared, and he slowed his pace. He had to find the source of the scent. It pulled him, leaving him no option but to follow. As both wolf and man, his sense of smell was always heightened, but this was on a whole new level. It seemed to filter through his olfactory channel, sinking into his body, swimming through his veins and becoming a part of him. All other thought fled his mind. Only one desire filled him—no, it was more than a desire. It was a need to find it. Something he couldn't control.

Carter set off again. Each step increased the intensity of the scent. It made him heady in a way he'd never experience before—as though he'd been downing shots of whiskey, or been smoking something he shouldn't. The pace of his heart galloped together with his paws. He was desperate to reach the scent, needing to know with every fiber of his being what created it.

He spotted something and skidded to a halt.

It took him a moment to piece together what he was seeing.

Fallen leaves had drifted across a bundle lying on the forest floor before him, partially obscuring it from his vision. Whatever it was, he had no doubt this was the source of the glorious scent that had overtaken his senses. He caught a glimpse of something pale peeking through the crispy brown, reds, and yellows of the fallen leaves. What was that? He took a step forward. Was that a hand? And yes, what he'd first mistaken as roots of some kind was actually a tendril of almost white blonde hair.

His heart stepped up a notch. Was the person dead? No, surely a body wouldn't smell this way. He'd scented death enough times to know it didn't smell like this.

Unwittingly, he growled, his upper lip pulling up to expose his canines.

At the sound, the fingers twitched.

Carter fell silent, his ears pricking. The scent of her had masked his usual ability to detect the details about something he'd come across. Normally, he'd have been able to tell a person's age and sex, if they were hurt or even in heat. He hadn't been able to detect anything about this one, though, his mind swamped only by his need to be near whatever smelled like chocolate and warmed brandy all in one.

A gentle moan filtered to his ears and broke his paralysis. Forgetting he was still in wolf form, he trotted forward and was able to get a better look. It was a girl.

She moved, as though trying to lift her head, but finding it all too difficult, collapsed to the forest floor again. She was clearly weak. Was she sick, or hurt?

Carter whined and nudged her with his nose. The wetness of his nose caused her to gasp, and he suddenly realized she would be waking to a giant wolf standing over her, most likely wondering if she was going to be dinner.

She woke and tried to scramble away. Her eyes widened, blue, framed with thick lashes, darker than the hair on her head. Her face looked elfin, with pale skin stretched across high cheekbones and a pointed chin. Her lips were naturally pink, with a defined cupid's bow. She wore a large smock which covered most of her frame, and smears of dirt marked the material. She was exquisite.

He whined again and took a step back, trying to tell her that she didn't need to be scared. Her eyes only widened more. So many questions raced through his mind. How old was this young woman? Not much more than early twenties, he felt sure. Where had she come from?

He wouldn't be able to get any answers to his questions while he was in wolf form. Though he'd been enjoying his run through the forest, relishing the quiet it brought to his mind, he had something new to distract him now. He didn't have to think about his own problems when he was able to focus on someone who looked like they had way more issues than he did.

The longer he spent with her, the more the distracting scent of her faded, allowing him to think again, though it was never gone completely. But with relief, he could tell she was like him. She wasn't a human, or another kind of supernatural. The girl was a wolf shifter, too.

She was in the middle of nowhere, and, though from the scent of her, he knew she was a shifter, he didn't recognize her from any surrounding packs. How had she gotten all the way out here on her own?

Carter took a couple of steps back. She'd managed to push herself to sitting now, and was watching him with wide, wary eyes. He lowered his head, and, with a growl, pushed away his wolf. His human form pushed outward, absorbing his wolf's fur, and his body changed shape. The change was fast—only a matter of seconds—and was as easy to him as shedding the day's clothes before climbing into bed.

As a shifter herself, he knew this change wouldn't frighten her. It did, however, leave him utterly naked. He'd abandoned his clothes back near the bike, where he'd first changed to wolf. Normally, his nudity wouldn't have bothered him. Carter knew he looked good naked. He was bulked with muscle and with barely an ounce of fat on him, and his tan skin looked as though it had been glued directly to the muscles of his abdominals and pectorals. But for once he worried that this young woman would find him more frightening than sexy.

To cover his cock, he dropped to a crouch beside her, his thigh and forearm covering that part of himself. He reached out to her, but she reared back.

"It's okay." His voice was low, soothing, like he was talking to a wild animal. "I'm here to help you. Can you stand?"

She hesitated for a moment, her blue gaze flicking across him and over his shoulder to the area behind him, perhaps wondering if it was possible to make a bolt for it, or maybe wondering if he had others with him.

But then she shook her head.

"You can't walk?" he prompted. Could she speak? Did she even understand English?

"Too weak," she managed. Her voice was as fragile as a dew studded cobweb in the early morning.

"You're too weak to walk?"

The girl nodded, strands of her white blonde hair falling over her face, her gaze slipping away from him as though her limitations embarrassed her.

He had no choice but to get back to his feet, but then he stooped again and scooped his hands beneath her body. Almost automatically, her arms seemed to find their way around his neck, holding on, so he was able to lift her from the forest floor. He held her against his torso, cradled in his arms. The oversized smock she wore protected her body from his nakedness.

She was heavier than she looked, her weight surprising him, but he was strong and fit, and he'd easily carry her back to where his bike waited. What he was about to do suddenly dawned on him. It was as though he'd been acting purely instinctively, with no conscious thought to his actions. He'd been fully intending on taking her home. Was that the right thing to do? What else could he do with her? She didn't look as though she was hurt or injured, and, being a shifter, he didn't want to take her to a regular hospital anyway. With her shifter genetics, she should recover from whatever had caused her exhaustion quickly enough without needing medical intervention.

She didn't fight him, or question what he was doing. He glanced at the ground quickly, checking she hadn't left anything behind, but there was nothing. Did she not have a purse or anything with her? It didn't matter. There would be time for questions later. He needed to get her home. He couldn't put his finger on it, but for some reason, the idea of her being out in the middle of the forest, weak and defenseless, did strange things to his insides. It didn't feel right.

He set off at a fast walk, holding her firmly against him.

He glanced down into her face, and found her staring up at him with those wide blue eyes.

"What's your name?" he asked.

"Piper," the girl said. "My name is Piper."

# Chapter Four

PIPER DIDN'T KNOW HOW many days had passed since she'd run from her home town in the middle of the night. Since then, she'd done everything within her power to put as many miles as possible between her and that place. Despite being aware of the dangers, she'd hitchhiked, run, walked, dragged herself along when exhaustion had gotten too much for her. She'd used what little money she had to catch a bus as far as she could afford to go, but after that she'd been reliant on her own feet and the pity of strangers. She had no plans for where she'd end up, only that she wanted to get as far away as possible.

She gazed up at the man cradling her in his big, muscular arms. From the angle she was at, she got a perfect view of his strong jaw. He glanced down at her in concern, and she noted the green of his eyes. They were a beautiful shape, too, still wolfish even in a human face. His mouth was generous, his nose straight.

Her rescuer marched forward, not breaking his stride, as though she barely weighed anything at all. She wondered momentarily if she should be frightened. She didn't know this man and, from the size of him, he could crush her in an instant. He could take her, break her, use her any way he wished. They were out here, in the middle of nowhere, and yet she'd allowed him to scoop her up and carry her away as though she'd known him her whole life.

"Where are we going?" she asked. Her voice sounded small, faint, and she didn't like it.

"Home," he replied, not even breaking his pace.

"Where's home?"

"Not far."

So he was taking her to his house? Again, the thought that perhaps she should be concerned went through her, but she felt safe in his arms. Able to relax for the first time in as long as she could remember. It felt good to give herself over to someone else for a while, and the warmth of his body seeped through the material of her clothes, warding away the chill of the forest floor.

Piper had reached rock bottom when he'd found her. If he hadn't, she doubted she'd have survived the night. Temperatures dropped below freezing after the sun went down, and while she'd managed to find places to hole up against the cold weather on previous nights, she'd never have had the strength to find anywhere for the night currently encroaching. As much as she'd been determined to run, the lure of the relief of just giving in pulled on her also. She was so tired—tired of everything—and while she wanted to fight for her future, she also wanted to sleep and never wake up.

A wave of fresh exhaustion flooded over her at the steady stride of the man carrying her, his rocking gait, the warmth of his body. She struggled to keep her eyes open, the weight of her lids dragging shut. It was crazy to fall asleep in the arms of a man whose name she didn't even know yet. He could be a murderer and rapist, for all she knew. But, in her mind, she'd left the danger behind her. Nothing could be as bad as what she'd been trying to escape.

Her eyelids fluttered open again at change in his motion. They'd reached the edge of the forest. Through the tree trunks, the gray of a road lay beyond. The sight made her heart stutter. Roads meant civilization, and civilization meant cameras, and phones, and computers. All things that could be used to track her. At least in the forest, she'd felt comparatively safe, but the forest was likely to kill her, so she had no choice but to accept help.

"I'm going to have to put you down," the man said. "I need my clothes."

She nodded, and he lowered her feet to the ground.

Concern glimmered in his green eyes. "Can you stand?"

"I think so." Just the small rest she'd had between here and where he'd found her had rejuvenated her energy. That, together with his body heat having warmed her, already made her feel better. She was a shifter and healed quickly.

He stepped away from her, and she couldn't stop her gaze from darting over to him as he strode away. His back muscles flexed as he moved, his ass a perfect, tight peach. Jesus, he was a beautiful man.

He stooped to retrieve a pile of clothing he must have left before shifting, and set about pulling on jeans and a t-shirt, shoving his feet into boots. She noted how he hadn't put on any underwear and tried not to think too hard about how the thought made her pulse quicken. It almost seemed a shame for him to get dressed, though she had to admit it was easier to think without all that bare skin on display. Not that she'd been in much of a state to think about anything when he'd found her.

He gestured to the machine propped up beneath a tree. "That's my bike."

"Bike?"

"Yeah. It's how I get around. Well, that and by wolf, of course."

"Of course." She'd never been on a motorcycle before. Nerves tumbled around her stomach. She must have lost her mind, but she needed help, and this man was offering it to her. She wasn't too proud to turn it down. One night of rest, and maybe even a good meal, if she was lucky, and she'd be on her way again.

The man swung his leg over the seat, getting himself into position, and then roared the bike to life.

She hesitated. "I don't even know your name."

He twisted to look over his shoulder at her, his fingers still gripping the handlebars. "It's Carter." He jerked his head. "C'mon. I'm not gonna hurt you."

"I bet that's what all the crazies say," she replied, but in her head she knew that wasn't true. The people who'd hurt her the most had told her exactly what they planned on doing with her. Even so, she found her feet moving forward, and, before she could talk herself out of it, she'd climbed onto the back, behind the man she now knew was called Carter.

"You're gonna have to hold on," he told her, shouting above the roar of the bike. "Don't worry. I don't bite."

She wasn't so sure about that, but it wasn't as though she had a whole heap of options.

Piper wrapped her arms around his waist, the hard muscle of his abs beneath his t-shirt pressing against her palms. Even though he'd been carrying her while he was completely naked only minutes before, somehow this felt more intimate. She edged her bottom away on the seat, not wanting to press up against him, knowing he might detect her secret. He might have realized it already, despite her baggy clothes—after all, he'd been carrying her this whole way—but, if he had, he hadn't mentioned it yet.

Before she'd even caught her breath, the bike was moving. She tightened her hold on Carter, hunching into him the best she could. Her heart thumped, and she clung to him as he navigated the rough terrain out onto the road. The reverberations of the bike pulsed through her thighs and core, and she prayed it wouldn't have any negative effects.

The bike took them down a narrow road with the forest on both sides, and no sidewalk. Within fifteen minutes, the road had widened, and a couple of other vehicles passed them in the opposite direction. They passed a homestead, and then another. On the side of the road was a signpost.

*Welcome to Silver Creek: Population 98.*

They were heading into a small town. They drove through Main Street, which contained a grocery store, a barber, and a coffee shop. She wondered how they stayed afloat with such a tiny population, but it looked as though they got by.

Carter turned off Main Street and navigated a couple of blocks. The plots of land were large, with maintained yards, and tidy, whitewashed houses.

When he'd reached what seemed to be the outskirts of town, he pulled over and killed the engine. "We're here."

He climbed off the bike and put out a hand to help her off. She took it, his fingers warm and firm. "Thanks."

She took in the sight of the house they approached, and her jaw dropped. Unlike the more modest houses they'd passed on their way, this place was a mansion. A pillared walkway surrounded the house. Tall windows graced the frontage—she counted ten windows on this side of the house alone. Topiary shrubs took position in huge pots either side of the grand front door. This town was small, but this house dwarfed everything else.

It was clear this was the alpha's home, which she assumed meant the man beside her now was also the alpha.

From the way he moved, she got the impression he didn't want anyone else to see her. He ushered her forward, using his body to block her from the rest of the road. He was twice her size, so it was easy enough for him to do. Perhaps she should care more—that maybe he planned on doing something with her he didn't want others to know about—but staying hidden worked for Piper. She didn't want anyone to know she was here either.

Carter leaned past her to unlock the door, and then pushed it open. She stepped inside first, glancing around with curiosity. He moved in behind her, pushing the door shut, closing off the outside world. Though she was inside a house with a strange man, Piper allowed herself to breathe. Though he was big and assertive, he didn't seem intimidating or threatening. She imagined he could be, if he wanted, but so far he'd been nothing but kind to her.

"Come through, into the kitchen," he said, already walking away. "I'll make you something warm to drink, and food as well. You hungry? You look hungry."

She nodded, following him. "Starving."

"Great, I'll make you something." He gave his head a slight shake, as though mentally correcting himself. "I mean, great, because I like to cook. Not great because you're starving."

She gave an unsure smile. "Okay."

"And I can find you some clothes to change into," he said. "What you're wearing is covered in mud."

A spurt of adrenaline fired through her. Clothes? Women's clothes? Did that mean a woman lived here? She hadn't given any thought to the possibility this man might be mated already and have wolf pups of his own. She didn't know why she had assumed he was single the moment she saw him. Perhaps it was instinct, or maybe it was wishful thinking. No, she couldn't think like that. It was the very last thing she needed. She'd only just escaped one man; she didn't intend on replacing him with another. Besides, considering her current situation, such a thing was impossible.

Even so, she found she couldn't stop herself from asking. "Your mate's clothes?"

He stared at her in confused disbelief. "Mate?" Then what she was thinking must have dawned on him as he gave a laugh. "No. No mate. This has been my family's home for generations. I still have some of my mother's clothes bundled away somewhere." He glanced her up and down. "They'll be far too large for you, but at least they'll be dry and clean."

Piper didn't mind. Large was good. She needed them to be large, and all the running she done over the past few days with no change of clothing left her feeling horrible. If she lifted her arms, she was sure she could smell her own body odor.

"Sit." He nodded at the round wooden table in the middle of the kitchen. "It won't be a minute."

She did as he'd instructed, slipping into one of the chairs.

Carter set about warming something up on the stove, and within minutes the scent of carrots, onions, and bay leaves filled the air.

"It's just leftover stew," he said over his shoulder, making it sound like an apology.

Her stomach gurgled with hunger. "Smells incredible."

He shrugged. "It's nothing."

When it was warmed through, he set some in a bowl and placed it in front of her at the table. He laid a spoon down beside it.

"Thank you." She picked up the spoon and scooped up some of the beef, vegetables, and gravy and brought it to her mouth. It tasted as good as it smelled, and she was so hungry, she couldn't even bring herself to be embarrassed about wolfing down mouthful after mouthful, while Carter stood and watched her with a kind of amused pleasure.

"I'll run you a bath," he said when she'd finished.

Her cheeks heated. He must have been able to smell her. With his shifter sense of smell, there was no way he wouldn't. How mortifying. A part of her wanted to curl up and give in, just sleep forever and forget any of this was happening to her, but she couldn't. Anyway, she'd already done the hard part. Now she needed to look forward and figure out what the hell she was going to do with the rest of her life. That was, of course, assuming *he* didn't catch up with her.

Carter continued, unaware of her thoughts. "And you can stay in the guest suite until you're feeling yourself again."

"You don't need to do this, you know?" she said, looking up at him.

"Do what?"

"Help me."

He shrugged. "Yeah, I know. Anyway, I'm not doing this purely for you." He gave her a wink. "Maybe I like having someone else in the house again. It's too big for one person to be knocking around."

"What do you do to be able to afford a place like this?" She'd meant to think it, rather than say it, and her cheeks burned when she realized she'd asked the question out loud. It wasn't any of her business. She flapped her hand. "Sorry, you don't have to answer that."

But he laughed, a smile spreading across his handsome face. "Can't say I can take much credit. The house has been in my family for generations now, and I invest what money I inherited after my parents died. It wasn't a huge amount, but I guess I have an eye for what's going to do well on the stock market." He paused and then asked, "How about you?"

His question flustered her. "Oh, me? Nothing, really. I haven't quite figured that part out yet."

She couldn't tell him the truth. A sickening darkness twisted her gut at the thought. None of it had been her fault, but she knew how it made her look—pathetic, weak, stupid. She was ashamed she'd been so easily pushed into something she hadn't wanted, ashamed her parents had seen her as more of a commodity than a daughter whose happiness they cherished. If her own parents hadn't been able to love her, then how could she expect anyone else to?

# Chapter Five

CARTER COULDN'T EXPLAIN why he felt a drive to help her. It was more than that. In his mind, there had been no question that he'd do whatever it took to make sure this beautiful young woman stayed safe. He felt as though he'd stumbled across some rare and endangered creature, and instantly recognized it was his life's work to make sure she was protected in every way.

His fingers itched with the urge to run them across her pale skin, to pause at her mouth and trace the line of her cupid's bow. But normally, where he would have simply pushed her up against a wall and claimed her mouth with his own, he didn't feel he could do that with Piper. There was something different about her, and it wasn't just the scent of her that made his mind blurry with an emotion he couldn't yet pin down. All the women he knew wore tight fitted jeans, showing off their sexy curves, yet Piper wore a loose smock, which covered her from head to toe. Was it a religious thing? Had she escaped some kind of cult where she wasn't allowed to show her skin?

He wanted to ask, but just as he felt he couldn't touch her, as though she was somehow on another level to him, he also instinctively knew he had to give her time to unravel, like the petals of a flower unfurling to the light.

And he had to be that light.

The house was plenty big enough for her to have her own space. He didn't know what he was thinking—that he'd make her not want to leave? What would the rest of the town think when they discovered he'd brought a strange woman into his home, and into their pack? He couldn't keep her a secret, could he? That was madness. No, already she seemed stronger since he'd found her in the forest. As shifters, their resources were better than a human's, and they recovered faster. By morning, she was sure to want to leave and continue with her life.

He guided her up the stairs, toward the guest suite. Though he'd carried her in his arms while naked through the forest, now she seemed more herself, he had to clench his fists at his sides in order to stop himself from placing his palm against the small of her back and guiding her up.

He reached past her to open the door to the bedroom of the guest suite. Though he rarely had guests, it was already set up. Carter crossed the room to the adjoining door and pushed it open to reveal a luxurious bathroom with a full sized bath. Without asking if it was what she wanted, somehow knowing it would help make her feel better, he ran the hot water and added a healthy dash of bubble bath. Steam and a fragrant scent filled the room, and he glanced over his shoulder to see Piper watching him. Tears shimmered in her blue eyes, and his chest tightened.

"What's wrong?"

She shook her head. "Nothing's wrong. I've just never had anyone do anything for me before."

Carter frowned. "What are you talking about? Me running you a bath?"

She sniffed. "Yeah, that, and the food you made me."

"No one's ever made you food before?"

"Maybe as a child, but as soon as I was able to, I fended for myself. I've always been the one to look after everyone else since then."

Sadness at her story filled him, only increasing his need to see her safe and happy. This was a new experience for him. He had never wanted to take care of another person before, not really. There had always been an ulterior motive—mostly wanting to get a woman into bed, giving her the impression he was an all-around decent guy, when really all he was thinking about was what was in her panties.

"Where are all your belongings?" he asked. "Your bag? A purse, even?"

Piper shook her head. "I had a bag, but it was stolen."

"Shit. Shouldn't you report it?"

Her teeth dug into her lower lip. "I can't."

He frowned. "Why not?"

"It's hard to explain. I just don't want the cops involved."

He cocked an eyebrow. "You don't look like a criminal."

His comment surprised a small laugh from her. "No, I'm not. I promise. Please, trust me when I say I don't want the cops around."

Carter nodded. It wasn't his place to push her any further. She had nothing to do with him. Just because he'd offered to help her out didn't give him the right to pry into her life. He assumed she'd get herself rested and warmed up, and then she'd be on her way.

His chest tightened at the thought. He'd lose that incredible scent.

"Well, you can have whatever you need from here. Stay as long as you want."

He watched her hesitate.

"My life is complicated, Carter. You don't need to be so kind to me. You don't know me, and I don't know you. We just met."

He lifted both hands in a surrender gesture. "Hey, all I meant was that you have a safe place here if you need it. No pressure. I'll leave you to it. Take a bath, and I'll put those clean clothes outside your door, then get some rest. You can do whatever you decide is best in the morning."

She passed by him, heading toward the bath, as he moved to leave the room. Then she stopped, and stood on tiptoes, and kissed his cheek. The scent of her washed over him, and he couldn't stop his body's primal reaction to having her so close. But then she pulled away again, leaving him only with a desire for more.

"Thanks, Carter."

"No problem, Piper."

He forced himself to leave, trying not to think of her slipping the dirty smock from her body, leaving her gloriously naked in the steam-filled room. He tried not to think about how her breasts would look in the bath, the nipples peeping out of the bubbles as they floated, unhindered by gravity.

He shook the thought from his head and went to what used to be his parents' old bedroom. He still had their clothes hung up in the closet and filling the drawers. He probably should get rid of it all—it had been ten years now—but the house was big enough that he didn't need to use the room. It seemed to him that no harm came from letting things stay just as they had been when they died. His father hadn't wanted to get rid of any of his mother's clothing during the two years after she'd passed, so it had never felt right that he clear things out either.

Carter selected a number of items from his mother's belongings and took them back to the guest suite. He hesitated outside of the door, not wanting to open it if Piper was in the bath. Instead, he placed the clothes on the floor outside the door, figuring she'd find them when she was ready.

The doorbell rang, and he hurried downstairs. Had someone spotted him arriving home with a strange woman on the back of his bike, and was here to ask questions? He didn't know how he was going to explain what he was doing to someone who'd want to throw a little common sense into the situation. Picking up strange women in the forest and bringing them home wasn't something that happened every day.

He opened the front door to reveal the tall, lean, black-haired figure of his beta, James, standing on his porch.

"Hey." James stepped into the house without even waiting for an invitation. "I know it's getting late, but I've got some papers I need you to look at."

Carter glanced over his shoulder, wondering if Piper would appear at the top of the stairs, perhaps wrapped in a towel, but the spot remained empty.

"Papers?" he said, turning his attention back to James. "What papers?"

"The Evans and the Farmer families are looking to do a house swap. Gladys Evans says their place is too big for just the two of them now, and the Farmers are still popping out offspring. It seems like the sensible thing to do, but I need you to sign off on it."

"Couldn't it have waited until morning?" he snapped.

James frowned. "I was passing by. You normally don't mind. Everything okay?" Then he grimaced. "Ah, shit. You cut up about Kimberly? I heard the two of you split."

Carter shook his head. "Nah, it's fine. It's not like I didn't see it coming."

James's lips twisted, as though considering his alpha's emotional state. "Okay, as long as you're sure." He lifted the paperwork higher. "You want me to come back with these tomorrow, then?"

Coming back for a second time would only increase the possibility of him spotting Piper—if she was even still around by then. He reached out and took the papers.

"Might as well do it now, as you're here. Then I'm gonna get an early night. It's been a rough day."

James stared at him.

"What?" He gritted his teeth.

"Nothing. I just don't think I've ever heard you say you're going to get an early night before."

"So sue me."

He turned and stalked into his office before he could say anything else that got his beta's spidey-senses tingling. He slammed the paperwork down on the desk and snatched a pen out from the holder. He quickly scanned down the document. It appeared pretty standard—it just needed his signature as alpha to make it official.

Carter scrawled his name then handed the paperwork back to James. "Anything else?"

His beta shook his head. "Nope, that's it." His eyes seemed to search Carter's face, and again Carter was filled with the worry James would somehow guess what he'd done. "Sure there's nothing you want to talk about?"

"Seriously, James. I'm a big boy. I don't need a shoulder to cry on just 'cause some chick broke it off with me."

"Okay." He started back toward the front door. "But you know where I am if you need me."

Carter didn't honor his comment with a reply, and instead showed him to the front door then shut it on his retreating form with relief. The last thing he'd wanted to do was explain the presence of Piper in his home. He didn't know why, but he wanted to keep her a secret, as though letting the pack know would only break the magic of it.

Though he'd been telling James he was tired in order to get rid of him, he realized the toll of the day had weighed on him. He went to the kitchen to pour himself a nightcap, downing the whiskey in one go, the liquor burning a path down his throat, and then he traipsed back upstairs.

He went to bed, his head filled with thoughts about the girl, now sleeping, he hoped, on the other side of the house.

# Chapter Six

PIPER WOKE WITH NO idea where she was.

The usual surge of adrenaline at anticipating what the waking world would offer her sent her heart racing, and she sat up. She was in a huge bed, with numerous feather pillows surrounding her, and a warm, soft eiderdown covering her body. Gradually, it all tumbled back—how she'd collapsed in the forest, and how she'd been rescued by a big alpha on a motorcycle.

Her hand slipped down her body to rest on the swell of her stomach. She'd found a t-shirt and some sweatpants outside the bedroom door, just as Carter had promised, and while they were far too large for her, they helped to hide her growing shape.

How long did she have to go now? Because she'd kept her pregnancy a secret from everyone around her, she hadn't had any pre-natal care. With the shorter gestations of shifter babies, she guessed she had perhaps a month or so left, but it could also be a matter of weeks. The thought terrified her, but it wasn't the prospect of pain she was frightened of. She'd be giving birth alone, in a strange place, with no plan for her future. Her baby wasn't even born yet, and she already felt as though she'd failed him or her. The father was a man she didn't think should be allowed anywhere near people, never mind a small child, and she'd allowed this person to get her pregnant—well, not allowed, as such, but it had happened.

Beneath her palm, the baby pushed out a foot, or maybe a hand, pressing back on her. Piper's heart swelled with love for the child she hadn't yet met. She promised herself it was just her and her baby against the world, and as long as they had each other, it would be enough. Yet all the practicalities of having a newborn threatened to crowd her thoughts.

Fresh nerves tumbled through her at the thought of seeing the man who'd saved her from the forest. She assumed he was somewhere in this big house. Last night, it didn't seem as though he was in any hurry to get rid of her, but the light of day might have made him change his mind. Besides, she couldn't stay here. What if the man she was running from caught up to her? The thought made her lightheaded and sick. He'd kill her, she was sure. Would he wait until she'd given birth and take the child as his own, or would he beat her while she was still pregnant, and kill them both together? She almost would prefer the second option. At least then her child wouldn't have to grow up in that house. If the baby was female, she'd be subjected to being no more than a housemaid, and, even worse, if the child was male, he may grow up to be like his father.

No, she needed to keep moving, at least until she was no longer able to. When she had no choice, and the baby's birth was imminent, then she'd be forced to stop, but only for as long as it took her to gather her strength again. Anyway, the man who'd helped her didn't know about her pregnancy. He looked like the kind of guy who quite literally ate women for breakfast, and the moment he discovered she was unavailable to him in that way, she had no doubt that he'd throw her out.

SHE FOUND CARTER IN the kitchen, frying something in a pan.

He must have heard her approach, as he glanced over his shoulder. "Morning," he said, a smile tweaking one side of his full lips. His light brown hair was ruffled from sleep, and the start of stubble darkened his jaw. His gaze shifted to the kitchen window, which looked out onto the front porch and the street beyond, and he left the stove to pull down the blind, shutting out the view of the road.

Piper didn't know his reasons behind doing so, but she still found her shoulders relaxing at the privacy. She didn't know who was out there, who might catch a glimpse of her from the outside world and recognize her. It was highly unlikely, but they were still all shifters, and there was a chance the man she was running from had contacts here.

Carter moved back to the stove and continued to cook. Eggs and bacon, from the smell permeating the air. "How are you feeling?" he asked.

"Better, thanks."

He nodded at the round kitchen table. "Sit. Breakfast won't be long."

Her stomach growled at the thought. Though she felt as though she should be telling him she needed to leave, she'd been ravenous since becoming pregnant, and it wasn't as though she had regular meals lined up right now.

Toast popped from a toaster, and before she could even offer to help, he'd placed a plate in front of her, together with a slab of butter, and then set about filling it with scrambled eggs and crispy bacon. He did the same for himself and sat opposite, before jumping up again, clearly having forgotten something. He yanked open the fridge and pulled out a carton of juice, retrieved two glasses from a cupboard, and then poured them both some.

"This is great, Carter, seriously."

"No problem. I was making some for myself anyway. It was no effort to make extra."

Maybe not, but she was still touched that he'd thought of her.

They ate in a companionable silence. Piper purposefully hunched forward, using the shelf of her now much larger breasts to hang the t-shirt over the swell of her belly. How must she look to him—this barrel of her body with her stick thin arms and legs? She'd always been slender, and now she barely recognized herself. Not that she minded. She'd sacrifice her figure for her child.

She'd sacrifice her life, if she had to.

Piper finished eating and got to her feet, picking up her empty plate as she stood.

"What are you doing?" he asked.

"Helping to clean up."

He took the plate from her.

"It's fine." She tried to snatch the plate back, but failed. "I've got it. Honestly, it's the least I can do."

He shot her a stern glare. "Piper, yesterday I found you barely conscious in the forest. I know as shifters, we heal fast, but still you need to rest."

She shook her head. "No. I appreciate everything you've done for me, but I can't afford to rest any longer. I need to keep moving."

His brow pulled down. "You got someplace to be?"

She glanced away, unable to meet his steely gaze. "Not exactly," she admitted.

"Then sit the hell down and let me do the dishes."

Meekly, she dropped back into the seat.

Carter had his broad back to her as he spoke. "So, you gonna tell me who the hell you're running from?"

His words were like an electric shock to her system. "What?"

"You heard me. The only reason you'd have for wanting to get out of here so quick is because you're trying to run from someone. You wanna tell me who that someone is? I'm gonna guess an old boyfriend."

He was close to the mark, and her face rushed with heat. She stared down at her fingers threaded together on the table. "It's nothing like that," she muttered.

"No?" he said, glancing over his shoulder at her. "Then you gonna tell me what it's like?"

How could she tell him the truth?

He must have interpreted her silence for exactly what it was—her reluctance to tell him what was going on.

"Fine," he relented. "I was just hoping I could help."

"Why?" she snapped. "Why do you even want to help me? You don't know me at all, and yet here you are, bringing me into your home, feeding me, giving me a bed to sleep in. I don't get it."

He shrugged. "Maybe I just felt like you needed help and I should be the one to help you."

He was right; she did. But he had no idea what he was getting himself into.

"You don't want to get dragged into my mess," she said, shaking her head. "Trust me on that."

He turned to face her fully, a fresh light in his eyes. "So you admit you are in trouble?" Did he like that idea? Did the thought of trouble excite him? Perhaps he was that kind of guy—one of those who always went looking for it.

"Carter, please ..." She glanced away again.

He lifted his hand in surrender. "Okay, okay. I get it. It's none of my damn business, and if you don't want to tell me right now, that's fine, too. But you don't need to go running off anywhere. I can't help feeling you're not safe out there. In fact, from the state you were in yesterday when I found you, I *know* you're not safe, but you are in here. So just stay. I'm not offering forever, but one more night isn't gonna hurt. Get your strength back up, rest, and then you can do whatever the hell you want."

She had to admit the thought of spending another night curled up in that big soft bed, knowing there was no one around who was going to hurt her, made her want to weep with relief. Could she do it? Spend one more night here? Yes, it would increase the chance of him catching up with her, but it would also mean she could rest like Carter suggested, build the strength to be able to go farther and faster when she did get back on the move. The offer was incredibly tempting.

"Okay," she finally relented. "Thank you, Carter. I don't understand why you're being so kind to me, but I'd be stupid to turn down your offer of help."

A wide smile broke out across his face. "Good," he said with a nod. "Now, is there anything else you need?"

She almost sat back and put her hands on her belly, but caught herself moments before she did, realizing it would completely give her secret away. "No," she said, "you've already done too much, thank you.

"Okay, well, I need to get some work done, so make yourself at home."

# Chapter Seven

CARTER LEFT HIS KITCHEN and immediately placed both hands over his face, tilting his head back. What the fuck had come over him? When she'd mentioned leaving, he'd been filled with panic at the idea of her walking out of his home and never seeing her again.

Everything about Piper fascinated him, yet he knew nothing about her. He didn't even know her surname. He'd had to leave her in the kitchen because he didn't trust what would come out of his mouth next. When she'd talked about leaving, it was all he could do to stop himself asking her to move in. This was insane. He'd lost his goddamned mind. What kind of person found a girl in the woods and practically moved her in with him?

Who was the person she was running from? Anger rose inside him at seeing the fear in her eyes. If anyone tried to hurt her while he was around, he'd crush them into a pulpy mush. How could anyone hurt someone so beautiful? She looked fragile, but he sensed a strength in her, a determination. He watched the war on her face as he'd offered her the comfort of a warm bed. She'd battled with herself, knowing she should go, while wanting to take that comfort.

He hoped he hadn't put her in danger by persuading her to stay.

His office was his place of respite in this house. Most would choose their bedroom, but for Carter it was sitting in his big, leather chair, in front of his even larger desk. He fired up his computer and checked his funds for the day. He spent the next few hours moving stocks and shares around, investing in companies that looked promising and pulling out of those that were falling. Though he worked hard, he couldn't stop his thoughts going to what Piper might be doing. Was she back in the bedroom? His ears strained, trying to pick up on any sign of her, but she was quiet, like a ghost in his home.

Once he'd finished his own work, he needed to turn his attention to pack issues. As alpha, if there were any disputes within the pack, those issues were first brought to James, and if he wasn't able to sort them out, or if they were something of importance, such as something that threatened the security of the pack, it would come directly to him. Luckily, today it seemed there wasn't anything too serious—a dispute about money owed from one family to another, and a mating between two of the pack members.

He realized he hadn't thought about his own issues since finding Piper. Was that why he was so drawn to her? Was it because she distracted him, or was it because of something biological? No, he didn't want to put his hopes on that. He'd tried before, numerous times, and he was sure there was something wrong with him. He was too proud to go down the medical route, knowing it would make him a laughingstock of the pack if others found out.

A knock came at his door, and it cracked open, Piper's face peeping around the edge. "Hey, I brought you coffee."

The smile that had been so quick to reach his lips since he'd found her leaped to his face. "You didn't need to do that."

"No problem."

"Did you make one for yourself?"

She wrinkled her nose. "I'm not drinking coffee right now."

He raised his eyebrows. "No? How come?"

"Oh, just the caffeine doesn't agree with me." Color had tinged her pale cheeks. He took the moment to study her more closely. The clothes he'd found for her hung off her frame, and she had a strange way of hunching forward. He wondered if she had an injury of some kind. Had the person she was running from—her ex, he'd assumed—hurt her so badly?

She started to back out of the room. "I'll leave you in peace."

"No, you're fine. Stay. Please."

He didn't understand why he wanted her in his presence, but having her around calmed his soul.

"You're busy."

"No, I'm done. Stay, talk to me."

She gave a small laugh. "About what?"

"You. Where you've come from."

Her lips tightened. "A long way from here."

"Another shifter pack?"

She nodded. "Yeah, but one that's a little more old fashioned than this one."

"Old fashioned?" he prompted.

"Carter ..." She gave him a pleading look, and he could tell she didn't want to talk about it. Curiosity burned inside him. He desperately wanted to know where this beautiful woman had come from. Did she have family? How far had she traveled? What did she look like in wolf form? He ached to know every single thing about her, and yet she was a closed book. Yes, he'd found her and helped her, but that didn't give him automatic access to her life. He was genuinely interested in this woman, not only in her body, which, because of how she was dressed, he'd barely caught a glimpse of. Her exquisite face was enough for him for the moment, how her dark blue eyes were filled with sadness and pain. He wanted to know what was behind those eyes. What in her story had made her look such a way?

While he'd been lost in thought, she'd been looking around the walls of his office. She pointed toward the framed photographs on the walls, the portraits of his grandfather and grandmother, of his father and mother, and aunts and uncles. She turned a circle, following the numerous faces immortalized in the photographs.

"Are these all your family?" she asked.

He nodded. "They were, yes."

"Were? So none of them are alive?"

"No. I'm the last remaining Reed. When I die, the family name will die with me."

"Not necessarily. You might have a family of your own one day. You're only, what, thirty, at the most."

He laughed. "Twenty-eight, but I won't make you feel bad for thinking I was older."

"Sorry. But you still have plenty of time to have a family."

"I think if it was going to happen, it would have happened by now." The old darkness at his center rose like a cobra and lashed its tail. He pushed it down again, not wanting to give it any more thought.

She gave a small smile, awkward, as though she'd sensed his discomfort. "So Carter is your first name, not your last?"

He was relieved that she'd steered the subject away from having a family. "That's right. Carter Anthony Philip Reed. My parents obviously didn't think it was important to have a name that would roll off the tongue."

Her smile widened, lighting up her face. "I think it's a good name. Strong."

"Thanks. I don't even know your last name."

She hesitated, and something he couldn't quite read passed across her features. "Can we just leave it as Piper for the moment?"

"Really? So you know my entire, pretentious name, and I don't even get to know your surname. Doesn't seem fair to me." He was only half teasing.

She glanced away, her face pinking up. "Sorry."

"Hey, it's fine." He was suddenly panicked she'd use his prying as an excuse to leave. He needed to distract her. He glanced around the room to spot his chess set, the board folded into the box containing the pieces. He nodded over to it. "You ever play?"

She glanced over at the box. "Chess?"

"Yes, chess."

"No. No one ever taught me."

He got to his feet and crossed the room to the round table where the set was. He gestured to her to take the seat opposite from his, which she did, and then began setting out the pieces. As he placed each one on the board, he talked her through which each piece represented and what they were able to do.

"This is the king. He's the one you must protect at all costs. This is your queen, and she's the most powerful player on the board."

Piper caught on quickly. He helped her at first, pointing out different moves she could make, which at first made him feel as though he was playing against himself. But then she started to make moves of her own, and before long, she proved herself to be a worthy opponent.

The hours whiled away. They finished one game and started another, bringing in snacks from the kitchen to eat while they played. Piper was good company, quietly reserved, knowing her mind while not throwing any dramatics when things didn't go her way.

She hid a yawn behind her hand, but he spotted it.

"Sorry. You should be resting, and we've been playing for hours."

"I've enjoyed myself. It's been nice not to be lost in my own thoughts for a change. Focusing on something other than my own problems."

He understood exactly how that felt. "You can always tell me about them," he prompted.

She smiled. "Nice try."

"Okay, but I'm here if you ever decide you want a sympathetic ear."

To his surprise, she leaned across the table and placed a soft kiss to his cheek. The scent of her washed over him, and it was all he could do to stop himself from grabbing her by the arm and yanking her into his lap.

"Thank you, Carter. I don't know what I did to deserve having you find me yesterday, but I'm happy you did."

He turned and watched her go, both his heart and his cock aching. He didn't know either, but in a small amount of time, Piper had definitely made a big impression.

# Chapter Eight

SHE WOKE THE FOLLOWING morning with her emotions torn. She should leave today. Today would be her third day in the same place, and every moment that passed made it easier for *him* to find her.

But the thought of leaving this beautiful house, with this gorgeous, caring, attentive man made her want to weep. She didn't know if Carter was like this with everyone, or if it was just her, but it didn't even matter. In a matter of days, she'd gone from being terrified and alone, to feeling safe and cherished, and he was the one who'd done that for her. She didn't want to go on the run again, knowing her baby was growing bigger inside her every day, that every day brought her a day closer to when she'd give birth.

Wouldn't it be the safer thing to stay here?

The temptation lured her in, but it wasn't possible. Her belly was growing bigger, and it would be impossible to keep her pregnancy a secret for much longer. Carter was sure to notice. Besides, he'd definitely notice when she went into labor and a baby suddenly appeared. She couldn't put that on him. What the hell would a hot, twenty-eight year old, motorcycle riding alpha want with a mother and a newborn baby? The moment he found out she was pregnant, he would run a mile.

Or else he wouldn't, and would let her stay on, but only because he felt pity for her. She didn't want that either.

No, she needed to keep moving. Maybe Carter would lend her some money, so she could at least find a motel room when the time came. She'd make sure she paid him back every cent, though at the moment she had no idea where she'd get any money. She'd make it work, though. She had to.

Piper hauled her expanding bulk out of the bed, sad to leave it behind. She wanted to take a hot shower—she didn't know when she'd get another one. She locked the bathroom door. She didn't think there was much chance Carter would walk in on her, but she didn't want to risk it. Peeling off her clothes, she stood naked in front of the mirror. The bump of her belly was unmistakable now.

She missed shifting into her wolf form, but she couldn't risk being seen. Her swollen stomach would be obvious without any clothing to hide it, and what if something happened and she was forced to shift back to human without any of her clothes nearby? People would ask questions of a pregnant wolf shifter without a pack, and word would soon spread. She couldn't have the news getting back to him.

Piper took her shower, taking time to enjoy the fragrant soaps, washing her blonde hair, and finger combing the knots from the long strands. Her thoughts went to Carter as she showered, thinking of the wall of photographs in his office, all those family members now gone. Just like her, he was all alone, yet when she'd mentioned him having his own family one day, he'd shut her down. Perhaps he was one of those guys who saw themselves as a permanent bachelor. Hell, maybe he hated kids.

Once she was out, dried, and dressed, she stuffed the couple of changes of clothing Carter had found her into a bag she'd located in the closet. She hoped he wouldn't mind her taking it, though she felt bad even about that.

Stupidly, nerves fluttered around her stomach. Could she just creep out? Would Carter fight her about leaving again, or had she already outstayed her welcome? He might even be pleased to see her go and have his house to himself again. But no, she couldn't sneak out. He'd been kind to her, and she owed him the respect of saying thank you and telling him she was leaving.

Piper took a deep breath and headed to the bedroom door. As soon as she opened it, the heady scent of bacon frying and fresh coffee brewing reached her nostrils. Damn. That man was making her want to stay by his cooking alone, and he sure seemed to like his bacon. She'd lost her taste for coffee since becoming pregnant, though for some reason she still enjoyed the smell. A part of her couldn't wait to have the baby so her body felt like her own again, but every time she thought such a thing, guilt swamped over her. For the moment, the baby was safe inside her. Once he or she was born, they'd be exposed to the dangers of the outside world, and Piper was terrified she wasn't strong enough to protect them.

She headed downstairs, the bag clutched at her side. Carter was in exactly the same position as he'd been yesterday, cooking at the stove. She stood for a moment, appreciating the sight of his broad shoulders in his t-shirt, and the way his jeans molded perfectly to his ass. Her stomach flipped, and a surge of adrenaline pulsed through her. She'd never been attracted to a man in such a way before. The relationship she'd been in had nothing to do with attraction, and he'd made sure to keep her away from anyone who might catch her eye. She was young, and a sudden sadness filled her that she'd never gotten to experience this, and perhaps she never really would. Her best years would be behind her, and soon she'd have a baby to think about, and she knew she'd always put her child before any man.

He glanced over his shoulder, and she did her best to wipe her thoughts from her face.

"Hey," he said. "How long you been standing there?"

She smiled, but the expression felt tight on her face. "Not long."

"I was gonna bring something up to you. Figured you must be still sleeping." His gaze dropped to the bag at her side and he frowned. "What's that?"

She lifted it higher. "I hope you don't mind. I'll return it the first chance I get."

His frown deepened. "I don't give a fuck about the bag, Piper. Why do you look like you're going somewhere?"

"I stayed the extra night, like we agreed. But I have to go now."

"You got a pressing appointment you need to be at?"

She shook her head, her face burning. "No, nothing like that."

"Then what's the rush?"

"I'm sorry, Carter. I appreciate everything you've done for me, but I need to leave now."

"Leave? Leave to go where?" He looked baffled at her insistence.

"I don't know," she admitted, sudden tears filling her eyes. "I don't have anywhere to go."

# Chapter Nine

CARTER DROPPED THE spatula he'd been holding into the pan and folded his arms across his chest. "What's the point in leaving if you don't have any place to go?"

The expression on her face—a combination of fear and hope—just about broke his heart.

"Because I'm too frightened to stay."

He frowned and shook his head. "Frightened? Frightened of what? That dickhead ex-boyfriend catching up to you?"

"He isn't just my boyfriend," she said. "He's my husband. His name is Finch Morgan, and he's a nasty piece of work."

*Shit.* Piper was married? He looked inward, searching his feelings. Did that make any difference? No, he didn't think so. She was clearly terrified of the guy—boyfriend or husband. Whatever he was, he didn't deserve her.

"I can keep you safer than you would be alone out there." He jerked his chin toward the front door.

She shook her head. "But for how long? I can't ask you to give up your life for me. You barely know me."

That's not true, Piper. I've gotten to know you over these last few days. I can't stand to think of you walking away from here, alone, with no one to look out for you." Another option occurred to him. "Maybe we should turn this around and I should go and find that husband of yours and warn him off."

59

Her blue eyes widened in fear. "No, please, don't do that. If you do, he'll know where I am for sure, and if he finds me with you, he'll be even angrier, if such a thing is possible."

"You think I can't handle him?" Carter tried not to be offended.

"I don't want you to even think about it, Carter. You don't know him. Yes, you're big and strong, but he's mean—mean in a way you can't even begin to understand. You might be tough, but you have a good heart. That man's heart is as black as coal." She gave a small laugh, but it contained no humor. "In fact, I wouldn't be surprised if his heart *was* just a lump of coal, sitting solid in the middle of his chest."

A click came from the front door, snatching their attention. The door started to open, and Carter froze. The irrational idea that he was about to see Piper's ex-husband walking through, as though talking about him had summoned him, went through his head. But instead it was Kimberly's dark hair he saw as she whipped through the gap.

She must have seen them both standing there, as she drew to a halt and her eyes widened in surprise. Her gaze immediately selected Piper.

Shit, he'd forgotten Kimberly still had a key.

"Kimberly," he said, "what are you doing here?"

She didn't answer, not taking her eyes off Piper. "Who the hell is this?"

He hesitated for a moment. It wasn't as though he could tell Kimberly the truth. There would be too many questions, and word would get around town that he'd brought a complete stranger into his home, and not only that, she was on the run from someone who potentially might be a threat to the pack.

"This is Piper," he said instead. "She's an old girlfriend."

Kimberly's fine dark eyebrows shot up even higher. "Old girlfriend?"

"Yeah. She's just come into town for a few days."

Kimberly's gaze flicked down Piper's body, and her eyes narrowed slightly, fine lines creasing her brow. Piper looked away, hunching forward, her shoulders rounding. Carter could see how awkward she was finding all of this, and he felt like crap that he'd unwittingly brought his ex into Piper's already complicated situation.

"You replaced me quickly enough," she sniped.

He pointed a finger. "Hey, you walked out on me, remember, and Piper is only staying for a while. Besides, what I do is none of your damn business anymore."

She gave a haughty sniff, lifting her chin. "I'm not interested anyway. I just came to get the rest of my stuff."

"You can leave the house keys while you're here, too."

"Fine."

*Sorry,* he mouthed at Piper, but she just shrugged as though to say it wasn't any of her business either.

Kimberly shot Piper a narrow-eyed glare as she stormed past and stomped up the stairs toward the bedroom. Carter knew he shouldn't be feeling bad in any way at having his ex-girlfriend suddenly appear at the door, but for some reason, he did. He didn't want Piper to see he'd dated someone like Kimberly—hell, they'd done more than just date. But Piper was the exact opposite, and not only in looks. While Kimberly put everything out there, Piper was reserved and quiet.

He hadn't done anything wrong, however. Kimberly had left him, and he hadn't even met Piper until later that day. Still, this whole thing was awkward as hell.

They both cast their gazes upward as Kimberly banged and crashed around.

Piper grimaced at him. "It ended well, then?" she said in a half whisper.

He shrugged. "It wasn't really either of our faults. It just didn't work out."

She nodded, as though she agreed, and he wondered how things had ended with her husband. He guessed *not well* would be the answer, considering she was hiding out in his house and afraid to stay in one place for too long.

Kimberly appeared at the top of the stairs, a small pile of clothes and books in her arms.

Carter stepped forward as she descended the staircase. "Let me help," he offered.

She pulled the items tighter to her body. "It's fine. I've got them."

Kimberly had barely even moved in here properly. She always kept enough for a couple of nights' stay, but it wasn't as though anything substantial in the property belonged to her. She'd not been here long enough to really put her mark on the place.

She paused before leaving. "I'm going to have to tell the rest of the pack about your visitor," she said, not even looking at Piper. "They have a right to know who's living among us."

"I won't be staying long," Piper added.

But Kimberly gave her a look that said she didn't care either way, and then turned her back and slammed out the front door.

Carter gave a sigh and turned back to Piper. "I don't know about you, but after that amount of drama, I could sure use something to eat."

To his surprise, she laughed and nodded. "Okay, sure. I'm hungry, too." He was relieved she hadn't mentioned leaving again, and, before they headed back into the kitchen, he noted how she dropped the bag she'd packed by the front door. Did that mean she was staying? He didn't like to ask again in case it prompted her to do the opposite.

The food he'd been cooking before Kimberly had shown up was a little dried out now, but it was still edible. He set out a plate for himself and Piper, and she sat down and started to eat. Things were easy around her. Where Kimberly was all fire and drama, Piper just seemed content to sit and eat her meal.

This time, when Piper offered to wash up, he accepted her offer, wanting her to feel as though she could contribute. He left her to it, needing to go and do some work. He hoped she'd still be in the house by the time he'd finished.

Just like the previous day, after a few hours, she reappeared at his door with coffee. He'd done everything he needed to by that point, so he nodded over to the chessboard again.

"Okay," she said, smiling, "but you're not allowed to help me so much."

"Nah, I wasn't helping you last time. You picked it up quickly enough on your own."

Her eyebrows lifted in skepticism. "You're a liar. A sweet liar, but a liar nevertheless."

He chuckled and got to his feet to move over to where the chessboard was still set out from the previous day. The movement brought him directly in front of Piper, but she didn't make any attempt to cross the room. Instead, she looked up at him, her blue eyes wide.

"I know what you're doing."

He feigned innocence. "I'm not doing anything." She'd picked up on his attempts to distract her from her thoughts of leaving.

"This will be my last night, Carter. I truly appreciate everything you've done for me, but your pack probably won't be pleased about me being here, especially not if I bring trouble into town."

He pressed his lips together, his nostrils flaring. "I'm the alpha of this pack. If I say I want you to stay, no one else can do a damned thing about it."

She shook her head. "But it's not going to make you any friends, and I don't want to be the cause of coming between you and your pack."

His heart clenched at the thought of her leaving. What was it about her that made him feel this way? He'd barely touched her—no more than taking her hand, or brushing the backs of her fingers, not since he'd first found her in the forest and carried her back. Yet he knew her leaving would take something from his life. She brought a kind of peace into his existence, a stillness of his soul. For once, he was thinking about someone else instead of what he wanted all the time.

"I can't make you stay, I know that, but there's a place for you here, if you ever need it."

"Thank you, Carter."

The way she was looking at him, her blue eyes so big, her chin tilted upward, her lips slightly parted caused a sudden urge to sweep through him. Without letting himself think about how it would change things, he slipped his hand around her waist and pulled her to him. Piper gasped, but he silenced her with his mouth, pressing it firmly against hers. Her lips parted, welcoming him, and then they were kissing, their tongues meeting, lightly touching. His other hand slipped up her body, wanting to get a feel for the figure she'd always kept so well hidden beneath those baggy clothes, but something wasn't quite right. Confusion flickered through him. He paused in the kiss, and then Piper pushed him away, spinning from him, her hand to her mouth.

Where he should have slid his hand across her flat belly, instead he felt a sizable curve that certainly wasn't down to weight. His mind tried to process what he'd felt, and he could only come up with one explanation. Still puzzled, he looked over at where Piper was standing, both her hands covering her face.

The words burst from his lips. "You're pregnant?"

She couldn't look at him. "I'm so sorry. I should have told you."

His mind was spinning. "Why didn't you?"

"Because I didn't want you to know. I thought that you'd feel even sorrier for me, and that you'd feel obliged to help me, when really you owe me nothing at all. This isn't your problem, Carter. You know that. I've just walked into your life, and I'm only going to mess it up from every angle."

He shook his head, trying to find the words, but he didn't even know what he wanted to say.

"The baby ..." he managed eventually. "Is the man you're running from the father?"

She nodded. "Yes. The pregnancy was the reason I finally made the decision to leave. It was one thing subjecting myself to his cruelty, but I couldn't have my child brought up in that situation. I knew if he found out about the pregnancy, he'd lock me in a room until I gave birth, and then he'd probably take the child away from me. I couldn't allow that to happen."

"So you went on the run, knowing you were pregnant?"

"I didn't have any choice." She glanced away from him. "But you have to let me go now, Carter. You see that, don't you? I'm not just some young woman who might be fun to have around the place for awhile. I'm going to be a mother soon, and you don't want to have a screaming baby messing up your style."

"I don't give a fuck about my style." He ran his hand over his mouth, thinking. "How long until the baby is due?"

She shook her head. "I'm not sure. I haven't had any kind of prenatal care. I couldn't let anyone know about the pregnancy."

"You think months? Weeks?"

"More like weeks," she admitted.

"Shit."

She gave a rueful smile. "Yeah, shit."

He grabbed her hand and pulled her over to sit at the table with him, though any thoughts of playing a game of chess had fled from his mind. "Well, there's no way in hell you're going anywhere now. You're staying right here, and I'll go and see our pack's midwife so you can get the care you need."

"You don't have to do that, Carter."

"Yes, I do. And if you even think about leaving, you'll have two men out there trying to track you down."

"What about if I agree to stay, at least until the baby is born, but I ask you not to tell anyone in town about the baby.

They'll start asking questions, and you know how close-knit the shifter community is. Sooner or later, word will get out, and it'll spread. If there's a strange, pregnant woman who's showed up with no connection to anyone, it'll get back to him, and he'll know where to find me."

Damn it. She had a point. Carter wanted to think he could handle some wife-beating asshole, but what if the husband showed up here with his pack behind him? This could start a war between two packs, and he'd be putting all his innocent pack members in danger.

He wanted to do right by Piper, but he also had a responsibility as alpha to keep his pack safe.

# Chapter Ten

"YOU DON'T NEED TO MAKE any hasty decisions," Carter said eventually. "Let's sleep on it tonight and figure out what to do tomorrow."

"Okay." Her voice stuck in her throat with emotion. He'd kissed her, and she'd loved how it had felt. She'd been so swept away in the moment, that for a fraction of a second she'd let down her guard, and by doing so had revealed her secret. She was stupid, so stupid, but her emotions were tangled. In part, she felt terrible for putting Carter in this difficult position, but she was also thankful to have un-shouldered some of the burden. Just as he'd been since she'd met him, he'd remained calm and decisive. She could see why he made such a good alpha for their pack, even if he did seem to pick up girlfriends a little too readily.

Who Carter dated was none of her business, but still her mind kept conjuring the image of Kimberly—sexy, feisty, with her long dark hair, and tiny, nipped-in waist. Nothing like Piper at the moment. Yet she and Carter had shared that kiss, and though she knew it could never work, she found her heart longed to experience that moment of tenderness with him again.

But he had kissed her before knowing she was carrying another man's child. Everything was different now.

"You wanna tell me exactly what happened?" he asked, his tone soft. "Why you're on the run when you're pregnant?"

Her gaze shifted away from him, but she started to talk. She owed him the truth. "The pack I come from is different than yours. It's old-fashioned, religious. The men rule the town—the position of alpha female doesn't even exist. The women are there only to be good mates and produce babies for the men. My husband was beta, so he was powerful in the pack. He and the alpha are brothers, and I swear everyone in the town worships them like they're gods.

"When I turned sixteen, my parents gave me over to him, like I was a gift to keep them in his favor. I'd only ever kissed a boy once before in my life, and I had no idea what to expect. He was our beta, and they were my parents. I cried every night when I found out what they had planned, but it never even occurred to me that I might have a choice."

Carter frowned. "But when you realized you were pregnant, you knew you had to make that choice?"

She nodded. "I had reached rock bottom. I knew I wasn't going to be able to live another day in the same house as that man. He did whatever he wanted to me, even though the feel of his hands on me, and his mouth on mine, made me sick. He barely let me leave the house unless it was to run errands for him. If I dared question him or speak back, he would hit me hard enough to knock me to the ground. I waited until he'd been drinking one night, and, when he passed out, I grabbed some of my things and left. I didn't let myself think about it too much, because I knew if I did, I'd talk myself out of it."

"What about your parents? Wouldn't they have wanted to help you if they knew how unhappy you were?"

She exhaled a small puff of air through her nose. "They didn't care. They only cared that their daughter was married to the beta, and that it raised their standing within the pack. I tried to tell them how cruel he was to me a couple of times, but they told me I was a grown woman now, and I needed to start acting like one."

"How long had you been running the day I found you in the forest?"

Tears slid down her cheeks, and he reached out and gently swiped them with his thumb.

Piper sniffed. "I'd been running for a few days by then. I only wanted to put as much distance between me and him as possible."

"Jesus, Piper, I can hardly believe it."

"It's the truth," she said sadly. "You must think differently of me now?"

He sat back, frowning. "Why would I do that?"

She shook her head, keeping her gaze cast down, not wanting to see the disappointment in his eyes. "Because now you know how weak and stupid I was. I let myself be mated off to a man I hated, and I didn't do anything to stop it."

"You were barely more than a child, Piper," he said, taking her hands in his. "There wasn't anything more you could do. It doesn't make me think any differently of you—hell, I think you're braver than ever." His shoulders squared and he lifted his chin, casting his gaze toward the front door. "But it does make me want to go and track the son of a bitch down and beat seven bells of shit out of him, though."

Her heartrate soared. "No, Carter, you can't do that. I already told you why. He'll find me for sure."

His green eyes had darkened a shade. "Let him. I'll kill the bastard."

"Please," she pleaded. "Don't make things even harder for me."

He exhaled a slow, steady breath, his shoulders relaxing. "Okay, but only because you've asked me to."

"Thank you." She bit on her lower lip. "So, what now?"

He shrugged. "I guess we just carry on and see how we feel in the morning. Sound all right with you?"

"Sure."

Piper didn't know how she'd feel in the morning. She knew she'd enjoyed Carter kissing her, and a part of her ached at the knowledge it wasn't going to happen again. It was a bad idea to grow attached to him, but he was gorgeous, and kind, and sexy, and she'd have to be blind not to notice any of those things. Plus, her hormones were running riot at the moment, which seemed to amplify all of her emotions.

They carried out the rest of their day like an old married couple. Carter continued with his work and then cooked for them both, while Piper tried to read a mystery book she'd found in the study. She struggled to concentrate on the words, and her mind constantly slipped back to Carter's offer to let her stay. She couldn't pretend she wasn't in heaven right now. She'd never imagined life could be like this—having a handsome man taking care of her, even though he knew she was pregnant and on the run with another man's child. A part of her thought she would be crazy to turn him down, but fear nipped at her heels, warning her that things wouldn't stay this way.

They always went wrong for her eventually.

# Chapter Eleven

CARTER LAY AWAKE IN bed, his forearm slung across his forehead, staring up at the white painted ceiling. He had barely slept the previous night, his mind turning thoughts over and over.

Pregnant. She was pregnant.

His world had shifted, his reality changing. Was that the reason he'd been so drawn to her? Had he, on some intrinsic level, realized she was the thing that had been missing from his life?

The baby wasn't his, but no one else knew that. He had a reputation for working his way through women. He'd already told Kimberly that Piper was an old girlfriend, and, knowing how Kimberly liked to gossip, that news would be halfway across town already. What was stopping him from telling people the pregnancy was the result of what was supposed to have been one last night together? He and Piper could easily have hooked up in another town somewhere, and the pregnancy was the result of that hookup. He'd tell everyone the baby was his, and, in return, he'd offer Piper and the child a safe home for life, and Piper would be able to get the prenatal care she needed.

The magnitude of what he was considering swept over him. Nausea coiled in his gut. This could change everything. Piper was the first woman he'd ever thought of in a way that was more than just sex. He cared about her. He wanted to keep her safe. Surely the baby was just a bonus? It would be the answer to both their problems. And if the ex came sniffing around, he'd tell him the same thing—that he'd met Piper months ago on a one night stand and the baby was his, and that was why she'd left to come to find him. It would keep the rest of the pack off his back, and give Piper a safe place to call home. It was a win-win on both sides.

Would she go for it, though? She'd seemed happy to stay, despite her initial resistance, but this was a step to a new level. They'd be deliberately deceiving people. He'd be lying to his own pack, and the idea sat uneasily on his heart. But he'd be doing it for Piper's safety, and the safety of her child, and it just happened to benefit him as well. Surely Piper and the baby being safe was more important than a white lie?

Knowing he didn't stand any chance of sleeping and with the sun already starting to rise, he gave up and got out of bed. He was so conscious of Piper asleep, he assumed, on the other side of the house. He didn't want to wake her yet, still needing time to gather his thoughts.

He went downstairs and made himself coffee. Now he understood why Piper hadn't been drinking any. He was sure he'd heard caffeine wasn't good for pregnant women. He felt so stupid he hadn't noticed before, especially considering he'd carried her from the forest. But he hadn't been looking for it, and she'd managed to disguise the pregnancy so well. She wasn't a big woman by any means, and her bump was small and neat. With a jolt, he remembered getting her to ride on the back of his motorcycle. He hoped that wouldn't have caused any harm to the baby.

Carter paced his house, the words he needed to put his proposition over to Piper dancing on his tongue.

Movement came at the top of the stairs, and he glanced up to see her making her way down. She looked sheepish, a small smile on her face, not quite able to meet his eye. She'd found some clothes that were a little more form-fitting than the giant t-shirts she'd been hiding her shape in, and had gone for a sleeveless tank top, which showed off her curves. She held her hand to her belly, and for the first time, Carter felt as though he was properly seeing her. He'd always thought she was stunning, but the way she'd held herself to disguise her bump had made her appear awkward, and something about her had always been a little off. Now he knew why, and he felt as though she'd taken shape before him. The roundness of her hips, breasts, and belly, and the way her white-blonde hair fell softly around her shoulders, only made his emotions for her grow.

Yet he couldn't bring himself to put his proposition across to her. Not for the moment. What if she turned him down? What would he do then?

"Morning," he said instead, falling into the easier option of what had become their routine. "Hungry?"

"Starving," she replied, taking the final steps to join him.

"Good." They went into the kitchen, and he set about cooking them breakfast—pancakes and syrup, with a side of berries and yogurt, food he assumed would be good for a pregnant woman. But he couldn't bring himself to sit down and eat, instead picking at the food while busying himself with the dishes before either of them had even finished. His appetite had vanished due to nerves, and he'd only made something to keep Piper's strength up and buy himself some more time.

Piper finished eating and got to her feet, picking up her plate to carry over to the sink.

She frowned at him. "What's up with you? You're pacing around like an expectant father." She gave a small laugh and gestured to her belly. "Which obviously you're not."

Her words were too close to the mark, and he couldn't help wincing at them. She must have noticed.

"Seriously, Carter." She put her hands on her hips, her fine eyebrows drawing down. "What's gotten into you? Don't tell me nothing's wrong."

He caught her hand and pulled her down to sit beside him at the kitchen table. "I've had an idea, and I want you to hear me out."

She must have picked up on the seriousness of his tone, as she twisted to face him fully. "What is it?"

He reached out and placed his palm against the swell of her belly, and the baby jerked beneath her skin, as though sensing his touch. He smiled at the sensation, momentarily forgetting what he was about to say as he was lost in the miracle of a life not yet born.

"Carter?" she prompted.

"Sorry." He removed his hand. "You know I've come to care for you over the past few days. You've been comfortable here, and happy. And it's been good for me, too, having someone around who I'm not in a relationship with—you witnessed the fallout between me and Kimberly. But you can't stay locked away in this house forever. The baby will be born soon, and people are probably already asking questions now that Kimberly has had time to spread the word. Members of my pack won't be happy to have an outsider live among us, and someone is bound to spot that you're pregnant sometime soon. Plus, you need to get medical help. What if something goes wrong during the birth?"

The hint of a frown appeared on her face. "What are you saying?"

"That we should tell people the baby you're carrying is mine."

She straightened, her eyes widening. "Why would you do that?"

"To help you. I want to protect you, Piper. And if that asshole of an ex shows up, we'll stick to that story. Say you met me somewhere and we had an affair."

She shook her head. "He'd never believe it. I never went anywhere. He practically had me locked inside the house."

*Much like you are here,* Carter thought. A twinge of uneasiness plucked at his insides like a guitar string.

"Okay, so maybe we can't fool your ex, but there's no reason he ever needs to find you. There won't be any rumors about a strange, pregnant woman showing out from nowhere because people will see you're with me."

Her teeth dug into her lower lip, and he could see she was considering his proposal. She hadn't told him an outright no, and said he was crazy, which was partly what he'd been expecting, so that was a good sign.

"But what's in this for you?" she asked.

He shrugged. "I like having you here."

"And a baby?"

"Hey, I like babies."

Her eyebrows lifted. "You do? I'm not even sure I like babies yet, and I'm the one who's about to have one!"

He laughed and reached out to squeeze her hand. "You'll be a great mom. Just look at everything you've already gone through to make sure this baby is safe."

She shook her head. "I don't know. I feel like if I was going to be a great mom, I'd have done more to make sure I wasn't going to end up in this position in the first place."

"None of that was your fault, Piper. I wish there was a way I could make you see that."

"Maybe I will, in time."

"So, let me tell everyone the baby is mine," he insisted.

"And we all just live here, like one big happy family?"

He gave a laugh. "Well, a small happy family, anyway."

Carter watched the struggle on her face, how she wanted to say yes, but was perhaps frightened of getting herself in another bad situation.

He leaned in toward her. "I'm not like your husband," he said. "If this doesn't work out, you're free to leave at any time. This isn't a prison, Piper. I want it to be your home."

She lifted her gaze to his, locking him with her blue eyes. Then she nodded tightly, almost as though she found the movement hard to do. "Okay," she said, her voice breaking. "Okay. Let's do it."

Carter pulled her into his arms.

# Chapter Twelve

OVER THE NEXT FEW DAYS, they fell into an easy routine—cooking, playing chess, her reading while he worked. However, the fear that her husband would catch up with her never left. She still jumped at the slam of a door, and lay awake at night with her heart pounding, expecting heavy fists to bang on the front door and for members of her previous pack to drag her home.

That Carter had offered her a home and shelter for her baby made her blood sing with happiness. It was a crazy idea, but everything about this situation was insane. She didn't know what she'd done to deserve Carter coming into her life, but right now she was more thankful than she could put into words.

Carter had made the announcement to his pack that Piper was pregnant with his baby, and the news brought with it a steady stream of people to the house to offer their congratulations and bring them gifts of things they would need for when the baby arrived. Piper hated that she was deceiving these people, especially when they were so excited that they would be getting a new shifter baby in their line of alphas, and so she made excuses about being tired or having a headache when people arrived, letting Carter deal with them.

The one person she did have to see in person, however, was the pack's midwife, Felicia. The older woman arrived with her bag containing a blood pressure monitor, her dipsticks for the urine tests, and a needle and syringe to take some blood, among other things.

"Carter tells me you haven't had any prenatal care?" Felicia asked Piper as she lay on the bed, waiting for the exam.

Piper shook her head. "It sounds stupid, but I didn't even realize I was pregnant. I guess I was just lying to myself the whole time. It wasn't until I found Carter again that I've really allowed what's happened to sink in."

"Well, obviously, that wouldn't be what we'd recommend, but we can't change the past now," she said, not unkindly. "From the size of you, I'd estimate you've probably only got another month to go."

Piper nodded. "That's kind of what I was thinking, too."

"Let's check you over and make sure you and the baby are healthy, then we can talk about birth plans."

"Birth plans?" she asked, confused.

"Yes, how you'd like the birth to go. I assume you wouldn't want to go into the hospital?"

Hospitals weren't a great place for shifters. They were mostly run by humans, and because shifter bodies worked so differently, normally shifters would either be able to heal themselves of their injuries or illnesses, or else they would die. There didn't seem to be any intermediate point, which made most of the medical profession obsolete among their kind.

Felicia ran a couple of the tests she'd brought with her. "All looks as it should be," she said, checking over one of the dipsticks, which showed the level of sugar and protein in her urine. "Now, how about I get a feel of the baby?"

Piper rolled up her top, exposing the mound of her bump. Every time she thought she couldn't possibly get any bigger, she did. Felicia placed her hands on Piper and palpitated the bump, looking off into the distance as she did so, as though she was learning things through her hands. "Baby is head down already," she said with a smile. "Do you want to hear the heartbeat?"

"Oh, yes, please."

Felicia took some clear jelly from her bag, and a piece of equipment that looked like a plastic stick. "This will be cold," she warned, putting some of the jelly on Piper's bump. Then she used the wand on the same place the jelly had gone, pressing down.

Piper listened with her heart in her throat. Irrational thoughts danced through her head. What if they couldn't find the baby's heartbeat? It was stupid, especially as she'd felt the baby moving only moments before, but she couldn't help herself.

Suddenly, the room was filled with the sound of hooves galloping, and Piper caught her breath.

Felicia smiled down at her. "Sounds good."

She looked up at the other woman with hope. "Really?"

"Absolutely. No reason why this won't be a perfectly healthy new alpha or alpha female for the pack." Felicia gave Piper a wink. "After all, he or she will come from good genes."

Piper forced her cheeks to tighten in a smile, when all along her heart felt as though it was being crushed. The baby didn't have good genes—far from it. She just prayed the baby would take after her more than he or she did their father.

# Chapter Thirteen

THEY'D JUST FINISHED up lunch when the doorbell rang.

Carter opened it to reveal his beta, James, and James' mate, Anna. They both stood on the porch, James with his arm around Anna's waist, and Anna holding a tin of what smelled like homemade shortcake. Carter had been fielding away members of his pack for the past few days, but he couldn't hide Piper from his beta.

"Hey," James crowed in a sing-song voice. "Hope we're not imposing, but we heard there might be something to celebrate."

Anna stepped forward and pushed the tin into Carter's arms. "I figured these would be more appropriate than bringing alcohol, considering the most important person won't be drinking." Her gazed darted around. "So, where are you hiding her?"

Carter backed up, allowing them both fully into the house. There was no point in trying to fight it. One person's business was the entire pack's business, and even more so when it came to the alpha and potentially the next alpha in line, too.

He glanced over to see Piper lurking in the doorway to the kitchen. He motioned her out.

"This is Piper," he introduced. "Piper, this is my beta, James, and his mate, Anna."

"It's nice to meet you," she said, smiling at them both.

Despite the lie, Carter's heart swelled with pride. She looked stunning, the cotton t-shirt and pants she wore showing off her bump perfectly. The moment he'd known she was staying, he'd gotten one of the other female wolves to go out and purchase a whole new wardrobe for Piper. He loved seeing her embracing her shape, showing off the ample curves of her stomach and breasts. He knew it wasn't his baby housed within her swollen stomach, but she still looked sexy to him. Ever since he'd first tried to kiss her, their relationship had remained platonic, but that didn't mean he wanted things to stay that way. If they got involved romantically, however, and he managed to mess things up, just as he normally did, it would make life difficult.

If only the baby inside her was actually his, and Piper was truly his mate, then his life would be perfect.

"I baked those for you to say congrats and welcome." Anna motioned to the tin Carter was now holding. "I figured you'd appreciate them more than champagne right now."

Piper laughed. "Yes, thank you."

"They won't be as good as mine," Carter said, throwing her a wink.

"Is he trying to fatten you up?" Anna teased.

Piper's smile widened. "Well, he does love to cook."

"And what more could you ask in a man?" Carter slipped his arm around her waist and leaned in to kiss her cheek, wanting James and Anna to believe in the relationship as much as the baby.

She gazed up at him. "Nothing more."

And his heart tightened.

"So, how did you guys meet?" asked Anna, the tone of her voice implying that she wanted all the juicy details.

"It's crazy, really. Just out at a bar. One thing led to another ..." He gestured at Piper's belly and they all laughed.

"I think we can guess what happened next," James said.

"Yep."

Piper blushed.

James clapped a hand to Carter's shoulder. "Then congratulations are in order. I have to admit, we were all starting to get a little worried that you didn't have it in you."

"Gee, thanks." He looked over to Piper, hoping she didn't suspect anything. A couple of lines had appeared between her brows, so he rolled his eyes and jerked his head toward his second in command as though to say, 'what can you do?'

"Well, it's good to know you've got an heir now," James continued. "Things start to get messy when we have to think about changing the alpha families. We could do without that sort of unrest, though I'm sure Liam and a couple of others will be disappointed to miss their opportunity."

Carter could feel Piper's gaze on him, the questions in her eyes. He gave an awkward laugh. "Nah, it wouldn't have come to that. I just needed to meet the right girl, that's all."

"Your mate," James said.

Carter looked over at Piper again. "Yes, my mate."

A small smile tweaked her lips, and he hoped he'd done enough. He didn't understand why he didn't want Piper to know about his need to provide an heir, and that he had failed so far. Hell, yes, he did. He didn't want her to see him how he really was—a man who used women to get what he wanted. Things had been different with Piper—*he'd* been different with Piper—and he knew that if she discovered who he really was, and that part of his reason for pretending the baby was his wasn't all about helping her, then she'd see him differently. He'd had his own agenda, and after hearing the story about how her parents had used her in order to elevate their place in their pack, he didn't want her to think he was doing exactly the same thing.

"I'll put some coffee on to go with the cookies," Piper said, turning away from the men to go back into the kitchen.

Anna followed. "I'll give you a hand."

Carter was relieved to have the moment broken.

James pulled him to one side. "I don't remember you ever mentioning a Piper before."

"It was a fling," he said, dismissively. "I didn't know it would come to anything—neither of us did."

"Feel free to punch me in the face if I'm speaking out of turn, but everyone in town knows you've had... issues... when it's come to..." He mimed the shape of Piper's belly onto his own. "Are you even sure the kid's yours?"

Carter growled in anger. "Yeah, I will punch you in the face if you start spreading those kinds of rumors. Piper's not like that. Have you seen her? She's as sweet as sugar, and anyway, the dates match up."

He lifted both hands. "Hey, no worries. I didn't mean to imply anything. I'm only looking out for you."

"I know that, but you know what the pack is like. Start making those kinds of comments and it'll be all over town before you can take a breath."

"I bet Kimberly is gonna be pissed about you cheating on her."

Damn. He hadn't thought of that. The dates would have been when he'd first started seeing Kimberly. Even though it was a fabrication, she didn't know that. He was right when he said she wouldn't be happy, and rightly so. They might be broken up now, but she'd still be hurt at the news.

There wasn't anything he could do about that now.

He shrugged. "Kimberly knew what she was getting into. She knew my history."

"And what about Piper?" he asked, nodding over to where she stood. "Does she know your history?"

"Not exactly, but she's met Kimberly, so that might give her a good idea."

He chuckled. "Right."

"Coffee's ready," Piper called from the kitchen, though he knew she'd have made herself a hot tea.

Not liking the line of questioning James had taken, he was glad for the distraction.

He could only hope the rest of the pack wasn't having the same ideas.

# Chapter Fourteen

AS THE DAYS PASSED, so her bump grew.

Piper learned her baby's schedule—the times he or she slept, such as when she was walking around the house, lulled to sleep by the rhythm of her body, and the times he or she was kicking up a storm—normally when Piper was trying to get some sleep herself. The rolls and flutters became less as the baby ran out of space, and instead were replaced by an elbow or a foot jabbing against the inside of her skin, producing sometimes crazy distortions of her belly.

Carter was out that morning on pack business. As her size grew, Piper found herself wanting to take the weight off her feet more and more. She felt as though the pregnancy had turned her into an old woman, and she caught herself groaning each time she got to her feet, and shuffling around the house with her palm pressed into the middle of her back.

A sharp knock at the door caught her attention. Though she'd come to believe herself to be safe since she'd been here, the thought of her husband was never far from her mind. She'd never let her guard down completely.

Cautiously, she went to the front door and used the spy hole to see who it was. To her surprise, Carter's ex-girlfriend was standing on the porch. Carter had taken Kimberly's key back, so she'd been forced to knock this time. What did she want? Maybe she still had more belongings somewhere in the house that she needed to collect.

Piper plastered a smile on her face, and pulled open the door. There was no reason the two of them couldn't be friends. Just because the other woman was Carter's ex didn't mean anything. After all, she and Carter weren't even properly together, and she remembered Carter telling her that Kimberly had been the one to break up with him.

"Hey, Kimberly. What can I do for you?"

Immediately, her gaze dropped to Piper's stomach, and instinctively Piper put a protective hand over her belly.

"So it is true, then," Kimberly snapped. "I thought there was something off about you the first time I saw you."

"Sorry?" she said, confused. Did Kimberly still have feelings for Carter? Was that why she seemed so angry?

"You realize you were fucking my boyfriend while he and I were still together."

She blinked in shock. "What? No, I wasn't."

"How else do you explain that, then?" She pointed at Piper's belly. "Because if it's true, and the dates are correct, then you and he were together just when we'd started dating."

Realization dawned, and Piper's face burned hot. "I'm sorry. I didn't know."

"He was only screwing around because he was so desperate to get a woman pregnant. You know that, don't you? It doesn't mean he actually felt anything for you. The only thing Carter Reed has ever wanted is a baby so he can keep his damned title of alpha, and this ugly old house."

Something clutched at her lungs, squeezing tight, making it hard for her to breathe. "What are you talking about?"

She gave a cold laugh. "You mean he didn't tell you the rules of this pack—that the alpha must produce an heir in order to continue as alpha? Carter has already worked his way through half of the females in town. You were just the one who got caught. It's amazing you did, really. There's been word around town that he's infertile. After all, half the women he wasn't able to conceive with went on to get pregnant with other males in the pack. It's surprising you got pregnant." She paused and then added, "Assuming the baby is actually his, of course, and you're not trying to trick him into taking on another man's child."

"Carter knows the truth about everything," she blurted. *Unlike me.* "I've never lied to him."

"Good." She folded her arms across her ample chest. "Members of the pack don't like to be lied to, especially not by some pale outsider."

Piper had heard enough. She took a couple of staggered steps back, and then reached out and slammed the door in Kimberly's face.

So, that had been the real reason Carter had helped her. She'd thought he cared about her, but she'd never come into it. It had always been about the baby. He only ever wanted the baby so he could pretend to the rest of the pack that he'd fathered a child. Had he scented the pregnancy on her when they'd first met? Was that why he'd been so kind to her?

Carter had tricked her. He'd promised to keep her safe, but that had nothing to do with him caring for her. He only wanted to keep his role as alpha.

Her heart thrummed, crawling up into her throat, and her hands trembled. Word would get around soon enough that

Carter's 'baby' most likely wasn't his, and then her husband wouldn't be far behind.

She couldn't stay here. Not now. And she couldn't stand to see Carter and hear more lies coming from his lips. She only wanted to get away from town and put as much distance between herself and Carter as possible.

Moving as quickly as she could, she hurried upstairs and gathered together the few belongings she'd acquired since being at the house. As a second thought, she went into Carter's office. She felt wretched for doing so, but she'd tried to be truthful with him, and he'd lied. He could handle loaning her some money after what he'd done. She knew where he kept a bundle of notes hidden in a pot, so she pulled them out and stuffed them in the bag. Piper hardened her heart against the guilt. People had been using her for so long, it was about time she started using them. And besides, she was heavily pregnant now. He couldn't expect her to sleep out on the street.

As a final thought, always with the fear that at some point her husband might catch up with her, Piper went to the kitchen and selected one of the knives from the block. She went for a smaller sized one, one she'd be able to move quickly with if she needed to, and added it to her bag. Not allowing herself to think any further, she let herself out of Carter's house. She didn't want to be seen, so she walked with her head down, though she was sure her bump gave her away.

She didn't know exactly where she was going, so she let her wolf's senses guide her. It wanted to go back into the forest, so that was where she headed. Her wolf had been quiet since she'd become pregnant, as though that part of her had needed to be silenced to allow her to concentrate on the new life growing inside her, but now, when it was needed, it rose to the surface again. She still had a number of hours of daylight—enough to get her away from town, through the forest, and out onto a road heading in a different direction. She didn't want to make it too easy for Carter to come after her. He was bound to realize what had happened once he'd heard Kimberly had paid her a visit, and discovered all her things gone.

Piper kept walking. She left the road and stepped between the trees, heading deeper. Her back ached, and she wished she'd thought to bring a bottle of water with her. Her mouth was already dry. Her stomach gurgled, and the baby kicked. Damn, when was the last time she'd eaten? Hours ago, now. She'd been so caught up in emotion that she hadn't planned this properly.

She'd expected too much from Carter. He hadn't owed her anything. He'd found her, barely conscious, and had done his best for her. But he'd had his own motives, and she couldn't stand the idea that he'd used her to his advantage. Her parents had done that with her when they'd handed her over to her husband, and the thought that she'd been used as little more than a prop hurt her heart.

Maybe she hadn't wanted to admit it to herself, but over the past couple of weeks, she'd started to develop feelings for Carter, and it was the idea that he wasn't the man she thought he was that hurt the most.

A sudden sharp stab speared her side, and she drew to a halt, gasping. She bent over as best she could around her bump and pressed her hand to the pain. Was it a stitch from all the walking? If so, it was the worst stitch she'd ever had, stealing her breath.

The pain faded, and she wondered if it had been as bad as she'd imagined. She was fine now, so she kept going. She wanted to make it to a motel before it started getting dark. Though she was healthier now than she'd been when she'd run from her husband—Carter had kept her well fed—she was also farther along in her pregnancy, and that meant she was moving more slowly.

A second stab of pain hit her in her side, wrapping around her belly to form a tight band. Piper gasped, the pain bringing her to her knees. Sudden realization about what was happening dawned on her. Oh, God. How could she have been so stupid? She'd been so caught up in the emotion of feeling like Carter had betrayed her that she'd only wanted to get away. She'd thought she still had a few weeks yet, but it seemed the baby had other ideas.

She glanced over her shoulder, back in the direction she had come. She needed to get back to town and ask for help, but could she make it? Once again the pain started to fade and she was able to move. On shaking limbs, she staggered to her feet. The pain had left her nauseated, her head spinning. *Don't panic, don't panic, don't panic,* she told herself, but it was easier said than done.

Piper only managed a couple of dozen steps back when the pain caught her, once more bringing her to her knees.

She wasn't going to make it back to town.

The baby was coming.

# Chapter Fifteen

CARTER PUSHED OPEN the front door of his house.
"Piper?"

He listened for any sound of her. Normally, she'd be in the kitchen, or reading in the family room, or even taking a bath, but the house felt strangely empty.

"Piper?" he called again.

He frowned, standing in his entrance hall with his hands on his hips. It wasn't like her to go out without mentioning her plans to him first. She still didn't really know anyone in town, and was understandably cautious about the possibility of her husband finding out where she was. Maybe she'd gone to see the midwife. She hadn't mentioned an appointment, but perhaps something had happened. An unexpected punch of worry hit him. He hoped everything was okay with the baby.

Not wanting to waste any more time, he backed out of the house. Felicia only lived a couple of blocks from here, and he'd be there in a matter of minutes.

He arrived at the midwife's home, out of breath, his anxiety increasing, but when he asked the older woman if she'd seen Piper, she only shook her head.

"No, sorry. She hasn't been here. Is everything all right?"

Carter bit his lower lip. "Yeah, I'm sure it's fine. I'm probably overreacting."

She gave him a reassuring smile. "Perfectly normal for an expectant father."

"Sure."

Leaving again, his confusion deepened. Maybe she'd gone for coffee with Anna, but then he remembered she didn't even drink coffee. What he'd told the midwife was probably right, and he was overreacting. Piper might even be home by now.

He picked up his pace, planning to head home as well, but a familiar figure walked toward him. His muscles tensed. It was Kimberly, and by the smirk on her face, he thought she might have some idea where Piper was.

They came face to face, both drawing to a halt in the middle of the street.

"Where is she?" Carter demanded.

Her eyebrows lifted. "Who?"

"You know who—Piper."

She shrugged. "No idea. She was still at the house when I left her."

"What were you doing at the house?"

"Just filling her in on a few details. Seems she didn't know about how you needed to produce an heir to keep your place as alpha."

His unease intensified. "What did you say to her?"

"Only that, and how you would have been cheating on me when you were getting her pregnant. I thought she deserved to know what sort of man she was having a baby with." The smirk grew wider. "Assuming that's even your baby, of course."

Anger surged inside him, and he clenched his fists at his sides, trying to hold it in. "You have no idea what you're talking about."

"No? 'Cause from the look on her face, I thought Piper had every idea."

He didn't want to get angry with Kimberly—after all, he understood why she'd be hurt, thinking he'd cheated on her, even though it wasn't the truth. He couldn't tell her what had really happened though, not if he was still trying to protect the story about Piper and the baby. And it wasn't only his part he was trying to protect. He didn't want the town to start asking questions about where Piper had come from either, or about the identity of the real father. Protecting her was more important than keeping his place as alpha.

The realization surprised him. Yes, Piper's safety was more important to him. For the first time in his life, he didn't care about the rest.

Leaving Kimberly standing in the street, he ran back to the house, blowing through the door like a sudden gust of wind, leaving it swinging in his wake. He took the stairs two at a time and hurried toward her bedroom. A quick scan of the room confirmed his fears. She'd taken the clothes he'd bought her, and the bag she'd been using was gone. Dammit.

Carter went back downstairs to the entrance hall.

He hesitated, unsure what his next move should be. Should he jump on his bike and ride around town, see if anyone had spotted her? But she barely knew anyone in town, and definitely didn't trust anyone else yet. Not that she should have trusted him. He'd not told her the whole truth, and he knew she'd be hurt and angry. No, she wouldn't still be in town. She'll have done what she was doing when she first came into his life.

She'd have run.

He needed to find her. She shouldn't be out, alone, so heavily pregnant. Anything could happen.

There was one way he knew how to find her. Her scent had been the thing that had drawn him to her in the first place, and he knew he'd be able to follow it again now.

Without waiting another second, Carter called to his wolf.

He didn't even bother to undress as the change began to happen. His body morphed into the shape of the big, black wolf, leaving his clothes in shredded rags. He shook the remnants from his body, pieces of material flying in every direction. He'd left the front door standing open when he'd come in search of Piper, so he leaped through the open doorway, a single bound taking him from the front porch down onto the street.

As a rule, the shifters didn't change while in town. Here, they lived almost as humans would, and it was only when they were back in the wild that they morphed into their wolf form. So, to see a large wolf bounding through the streets would have been a rare sight to the townspeople, and to see it was their alpha himself was sure to get tongues wagging. Carter didn't care about gossips at that moment; they could say whatever the hell they wanted. His sole focus was finding Piper.

The scent of her, that same vanilla and just-out-of-the-oven cupcake aroma that he'd caught on the first day, still spoke to him. It appeared in an almost visible track, like a jet stream across a bright blue sky. If she'd caught transport at any point, he'd lose the trail, so he prayed she'd remained on foot.

He moved fast, nose to the ground. She'd not headed toward Main Street, but had instead gone in the opposite direction, leaving the streets and houses in favor of the forest that surrounded them. As a species, they found being lost within nature soothing to their souls. It was only their human side that made them want to build walls and roofs to shelter within. Even in her condition, he guessed it was only natural for a shifter to want to be back with the natural world. Just because she'd not been able to shift and he hadn't even seen her in wolf form, didn't mean she didn't still long to be during times of difficulty. He hated that he'd been the one to cause her such upset.

He kept running, tracking her scent. Going into the forest reduced the chance that she'd caught a ride with someone. He hoped she wouldn't have taken the risk of crossing moving water. Not only would it be dangerous, he might also lose her scent.

She was heavily pregnant and in human form. She couldn't have gotten far.

His sensitive ears pricked, picking up the sound of gasped breaths and moans of pain. She must be close. He moved faster, his paws pounding the forest floor. Hot air snorted from his nostrils, shoulders bunched as he ran, his tail flat. His heart galloped in his chest. Something was wrong, he could tell from the sounds she made, and not just that. Her scent had changed. That sweet, vanilla fragrance was overlaid by something else. Something darker, earthier.

Carter came across her suddenly, forcing him to skid to a halt. She'd managed to find shelter against a fallen tree trunk, and now sat on the ground, her back pressed up against it. Her legs were spread wide in front of her. Her skin was even paler than normal, her white-blonde hair matted against her face with sweat. She was panting, her eyes wild in her head.

She looked up and saw him, and relief spread across her face.

"The baby," she managed between gasps. "The baby is coming."

He wouldn't be able to help in wolf form. Taking a couple of steps away, he lowered his head and willed his transformation back to human.

He was naked again, but that didn't matter.

Carter dropped to his knees beside her. "Shit, Piper. What can I do? Can you make it back to town?"

"No, I can't. No time."

"No time? You mean the baby is coming?"

She nodded, tears in her eyes. She looked terrified and in pain, and he wished he could do something to ease her suffering. She suddenly clenched her jaw and put her chin down. She grabbed for his hand, and, when she took it, she squeezed it hard enough to make him worry about bones shattering. A low moan emanated from the back of her throat.

Shit, that was a contraction.

"Can I get the midwife to come here?" he asked, trying not to panic.

"No, there's not enough time," she managed when she could talk again. "I can already feel the baby coming."

*Fuck, fuck, fuck.* He didn't have any choice. He needed to help her deliver the baby. He didn't think anything had ever truly frightened him his whole life. Maybe when he'd lost his parents, and had wondered how he was going to be alpha for the whole town, but even then it hadn't been anything like this kind of fear. He was terrified he'd do something wrong and hurt either Piper or the baby. What if he killed her child? How would they ever get past that?

He shook his fears away. Self doubt wasn't going to help Piper.

"We need to get your pants off, Piper," he said. "I need to be able to see what's going on."

She shook her head. "No, no. Don't touch me."

"I have to."

He eased his hands beneath her and carefully pulled her sweatpants, together with her underwear, down from her waist, over her bottom, and down over her thighs. He threw them away, and then grabbed the bag she'd brought with her. He found one of the big t-shirts she'd been hanging around the house in, and draped it across her lap to cover her modesty. He wasn't sure she even cared at this point, too lost in pain and fear to give any thought to what he was seeing.

"I need to see what's going on," he told her, pressing her thighs apart with his hands. She gave another moan and shifted down farther, spreading her legs and allowing him to see.

There was a swelling between her thighs, a bulge where there normally wouldn't be one. It was the top of the baby's head already. He'd thought he be able to see hair, but there still seemed to be a membrane around the baby. It was the waters; they still hadn't burst. The baby was about to be born still inside the bag of waters. He had no idea what he should do.

Piper gave another cry of pain, gritting her teeth and pressing her chin down to her chest. More of the top of the baby's head became visible as she pushed.

"It's coming," he cried. "The baby's coming."

"I know it's fucking coming," she yelled back when the contraction had passed. "I can feel every single inch of it."

Carter decided it was probably best not to say anything after that. He wanted to encourage her, but figured telling her to push was probably going to get a similar reaction. Instead, he waited, allowing Piper's body to do what it needed.

She had another couple of contractions, more of the head appearing each time, and then the baby arrived, slithering out from between Piper's legs. Carter tore the membrane from the baby's face, and was rewarded with a gush of water. He was sure it was supposed to be lucky for a baby to be born in such a way, but he wasn't concerned with that right now.

Already, Piper was recovering, sitting up to look down at the newborn.

"Is it okay? Why isn't it breathing?" she cried.

He used his finger to remove the rest of the membrane from the baby's face and quickly rubbed at the small body with a t-shirt. The baby was blue, but the moment he started rubbing, it opened its mouth and sucked in a lungful of air. On the exhale, a loud cry filled the forest.

Piper clamped her hand to her mouth. "Oh, thank God."

Carter looked up at her. "It's a boy, Piper. You have a son."

They stared at each other in amazement. Tears trembled in her blue eyes, and a painful lump choked Carter's throat as the enormity of what had just happened washed over him.

The baby was still attached to her via the umbilical cord.

"Dammit," he said, looking around. "I don't have anything to cut the cord with."

"There's a knife in the bag. I took it for protection."

He didn't want to think about how frightened she must have been to pack a knife, but he was grateful for it now. Way beyond any squeamishness, he cut the cord, separating the two of them.

Carter wrapped the baby in a sweater, bundling him up so only his tiny face peeped out, and then he handed the baby boy to his mother. Piper clutched the baby to her chest and burst into tears.

He pulled them both into his arms and held them, kissing Piper's head, then her eyes, her cheeks, her mouth. "I'm so sorry," he said. "I'm so sorry I didn't tell you the truth."

She shook her head. "Not now, Carter. It's okay, but we can do this later."

She was right.

He stared down at the tiny pink baby in Piper's arms, and then reached out and touched the child's fingers. The baby's fist opened and then closed around Carter's digit, such miniscule fingers with a strong grip and perfect clam-shells of fingernails. He gazed down in wonder, and then the baby opened his eyes and looked right back at him. Dark blue eyes exactly the same color and shape as Piper's.

And the alpha's heart ballooned with unexpected love.

# Chapter Sixteen

SHE'D NEVER BEEN SO relieved to see anyone in her life when Carter found her.

By that time, she had already realized she'd made a stupid mistake. She should have stayed and talked things out with him instead of running away. That hadn't solved anything and could have cost her baby his life.

Carter helped her dress while she held the baby to her chest. She thought she was supposed to try to nurse straight after birth, or do skin-to-skin contact, but none of those things was as important as getting them somewhere safe and warm.

She held her baby and Carter held her as he walked them back through the forest, toward town. She was a mess, her clothes bloodied, her hair damp with sweat, but Carter hadn't so much as flinched at the sight of her. Maybe he hadn't been completely truthful with her, and he had his reasons for that, but the way he'd handled things during her child's birth had shown her the measure of the man he was.

They walked back into town, Carter half-carrying her most of the way. One of the younger male pack members spotted them, his eyes widening.

"Go and get Felicia," he instructed the terrified young man. "Tell her to meet us at my house. Tell her Piper has had the baby."

The man nodded and ran off in the direction of Felicia's house. Piper would be glad to see the older woman. From the way the baby nuzzled and mewled in her arms, she was sure he was fine, but she'd be reassured to have them both checked over by someone who knew what they were doing.

They made it back to the house, and Carter helped her upstairs. Just as he'd done on the first day he'd found her, he ran her a bath. She knew there was no time for long soaks any more—not for another few years anyway—so dipped in enough to wash the blood and sweat from her body, while Carter held the baby. Already, her shifter genetics were coming into play, and she could feel herself healing. The blood flow had already slowed, her deflated stomach already beginning to shrink. It would take a few days, maybe even a week or more, but soon enough she'd be back to her old self.

She dared to think forward to the future, to when the baby was old enough for them to shift together. Long runs through the forest, teaching him to hunt, to be fast and strong, and a love she'd never experienced before surged through her. She glanced over to where Carter held the baby, and that love swelled to create a bubble, encasing Carter as well.

Maybe things weren't perfect. Maybe they were messy and complicated, but they were real, and that was what was important. She couldn't predict the future and know they would make it, and they both had a lot of talking to do, but she knew she loved this man.

She just hoped he felt the same way about her.

The doorbell rang.

"That'll be Felicia," Carter said. "I'll bring her up."

He left the room, leaving her alone with her son. She gazed down into the boy's perfect face, amazed that he'd been growing inside her all this time. She stroked his cheek, soft as satin.

"So, you're the one who's been kicking me, huh?" she said softly. The baby blinked back at her, and she realized she hadn't even thought of a name.

Carter reappeared with Felicia by his side. The older woman smiled kindly as she walked through. "Well, that all happened a bit fast," she said.

Piper nodded. "Yes. I definitely wasn't expecting to give birth in the middle of the forest."

Her smile broadened. "Our kind has been doing it for centuries. Maybe your baby wanted nature to be the first thing he saw when he was born."

She appreciated Felicia's kindness, not berating her for being so stupid and going out there alone in the first place.

"Now, let's check the little guy over."

She held out her arms for the baby, and Piper handed him over, already missing the feel of his warm little body in her arms.

"Has he tried to nurse yet?" Felicia asked as she checked him over.

Piper shook her head. "No, I haven't even tried."

"Well, he looks perfect. I think that's the best thing to start with."

Carter cleared his throat. "I'll give you some privacy."

Felicia turned to look over her shoulder at him. "No, don't be silly. It's perfectly natural for the father to be around while the baby is nursing."

Of course. The rest of the pack now believed their alpha had a son. Would she be the one to destroy all of that with a few simple words? She found she couldn't.

Piper nodded. "Yes, stay. We both want you to stay."

They exchanged a smile, and Carter stepped closer to take her hand.

Felicia handed the baby back again, and Piper released Carter's hand so she could rearrange her clothing to try to feed her son. She wasn't embarrassed to expose herself with Carter there—after all, he'd already seen far more than she'd ever had a man see of her, even the man she now thought of as her ex-husband.

She sucked in a breath as the baby's mouth clamped around her swollen nipple. Felicia gave her a smile of understanding. "It'll get easier," she reassured her. "It's always hardest at the start."

"Thank you."

"Now, I'll leave you to it. You look like you could use a little family time."

It was Carter's turn to thank her.

"You're welcome. I didn't do anything, really. You all did the hard work."

The midwife left the room, so they were once again alone. The three of them.

"What do we do now?" Carter asked.

She looked into his eyes. "What do you want to do?"

"I want you to stay." He nodded toward the small bundle at her breast. "I know this isn't normally how families work, but I can't imagine continuing my life with you not in it, and now he's here, too, it all just feels... right."

"I wish you'd told me about the covenant about you needing to produce an heir. Things would have made a lot more sense then."

A couple of lines appeared between his brows. "How so?"

"Because I could never quite figure out why you want to look after me the way you did, but then, when I learned that you needed a baby to keep your position as alpha, it all fell into place."

He shook his head. "That wasn't the reason I wanted to take care of you, Piper. The first moment I saw you, I was crazy about you. I didn't even know you were pregnant, and by the time I did, I had already fallen head over heels. Yes, I should have told you about the covenant, but I was worried you'd think I was using you because of the baby, and in the end that was exactly what you did think, and you ran."

She glanced away, ashamed. "I know. I shouldn't have run. It was stupid and immature of me. I should have stayed so we could have talked it out."

"But nothing has changed, Piper. You mean everything to me, and now, so does this little guy. I don't care about being alpha if it would mean losing both of you. I'll give it up, my position and this house."

Something bloomed in her chest. "You mean that?"

"With every inch of my soul."

She sniffed and nodded, and then he leaned in and kissed her, softly at first, then with more passion, ending with a promise that there would be more to come when the time was right.

"He needs a name," she said when the kiss broke. "Our boy needs a name."

"Any ideas?" he asked with a smile.

"I always liked Theo. What do you think?"

"Theo," he repeated, as though testing the sound of it in his mouth. "Yes, I like it. It suits our boy."

"A son," she smiled. "We have a son."

# Chapter Seventeen

DAYS AND WEEKS PASSED, and they fell into a routine of sorts, at least as much of a routine as it was possible to have with a newborn.

Despite her bitterness, Kimberly hadn't said anything to the rest of the pack about her suspicions about Theo's paternity. To the outside world, they looked like the perfect family, and, if it weren't for that little thing of genetics, they would have been, too. They'd had a stream of visitors bringing gifts for Theo, and though they'd only had the basics ready for him when he'd been born, within a matter of days he had more stuffed toys and clothes than he could ever need. The pack had also accepted Piper, though a couple of people were noticeably absent. Carter couldn't blame Kimberly for still feeling bitter, though he hoped Liam wasn't going to cause him problems. He knew the other shifter had had his eye on his spot as alpha, but now that Theo had been born, it changed everything.

He'd watched Piper grow into motherhood with astounding strength and grace. She seemed to instinctively know what Theo needed, and, at times where he was left pacing and rocking with the baby, asking him if he was hungry or needed his diaper changing—as though the kid could answer—she'd be able to swoop in and stop him crying. Occasionally, the thought popped into his head that Theo might understand that Carter wasn't his real father, but he pushed it away. Theo's real father was a nasty son of a bitch who didn't deserve either Piper or Theo in his life. He'd seen to that when he'd spent years abusing Piper, and there was no point where Carter felt guilty. If anything, the main thing Carter felt was anger, and only Piper's insistence for him to leave things well alone stopped him from tracking Piper's ex down and beating the shit out of him.

Carter had taken to sleeping in the bed with Piper, leaving his own bed on the other side of the house cold and empty. Theo woke them both several times a night, but neither of them minded. James stepped in to help with the workload, running the pack when the baby had been up most of the night, and Carter and Piper took turns napping.

There was affection between them, and they'd shared many kisses, but that was as far as things had gotten between them physically. After the birth, he'd kind of felt as though Piper's body belonged to Theo, and he didn't want to encroach on that until Piper was one hundred percent ready.

That wasn't saying he didn't want her. He wanted her desperately. He ached for her with every fiber of his being, but his relationship with her was more important than getting what he needed physically. He'd never done this before, establishing a relationship with a woman before they'd even had sex. Normally, sex was the first thing to happen, and then they figured out if they actually liked each other. Numerous times after they had shared a kiss and he'd forced himself to break away, he'd gone into the shower and masturbated furiously to get rid of his aching hard-on. But he respected her need to mother Theo.

She surprised him one afternoon while Theo was taking his nap. "What do you think of me?"

"What do you mean?"

"Am I just Theo's mother to you, or something more?"

Her question astonished him. "You're everything to me. Theo's mother, of course, but my world as well."

She held his gaze. "Then why don't you touch me?"

The muscles in his shoulders tensed. "I was leaving it up to you. I didn't want you to think I was pushing things too soon."

A smile spread across her beautiful face. "Too soon. Carter, how long has it been now? A couple of months? I don't think anytime from now could be too soon."

He placed his hand against her cheek, staring into her eyes. "What does that mean? You're ready?"

"Carter, I've been ready since the moment we met."

He leaned in and pressed his lips to hers. Her arms snaked around the back of his neck, and he wrapped his around her waist, pulling her flush against him. Just the mention of sex had gotten blood flowing to his cock, and there was no way she wouldn't be able to feel how much he wanted her pressing into her stomach. Not that he minded. He wanted her to see how much he'd desired her, how it had never been that he didn't want her, only that he'd been holding himself back, waiting for her.

Their kiss deepened, and Piper's lips parted, her tongue darting out to touch his. Desire shot through him, and a groan escaped his mouth. He'd spent so long imagining this moment, and there was nothing he would change.

He drew back, but only long enough to pull his t-shirt over his head. Then he was kissing her again, his fingers laced in the soft, silky strands of her striking hair. His fingers reached her shoulders, and he dragged both the straps of the sleeveless top she wore, together with her bra, down her arms. Her breasts spilled from the top, and he reached for them, finally getting his hands on the gloriously soft mounds.

He lifted her, his hands around the backs of her thighs, her legs around his hips, still kissing, and carried her to the bed. He dumped her on her back, with him leaning over her. Her hands traced the muscles of his shoulders and back, running over every inch of his skin, as though she was blind and trying to see him through her hands. He was already addicted to her touch, knowing he wanted to feel her fingers against his skin for the rest of his life.

He ducked his head to her swollen breasts, the big, milky nipples, the pale skin with lines of blue veins close beneath the surface. He circled her nipple with his tongue, feeling the large areola crinkle beneath his caress, and then sucked the hardened nub into his mouth, tasting her milk on his palate. She was incredible. Beautiful, sexy, and had gone through so much to give her child a life. He laved her nipple with his tongue, using his hand to massage her other breast with his hand, squeezing and rolling, before moving his mouth over and repeating. Piper moaned, her back arching, pressing her breasts up for his administrations. He loved hearing those sounds coming from her mouth, and knowing he was the one to cause them.

He lifted his mouth from her, rolled her top off fully, and then got to work on her jeans. He popped the button and yanked them from her hips, leaving her in only her panties. Then a thought went through his head, and he paused.

"Are you...? He didn't know how to ask without completely ruining the moment.

She took his hand and guided it down. "It's okay, Carter. We heal fast, remember? Same goes for childbirth. I'm good as new."

She half sat to pull his face toward hers, and she kissed him this time, her mouth hungry for him. She was so beautiful and he wanted her so badly, all trepidation fled his mind. He slid his hand across her stomach, down beyond the waistband of her panties. His fingers slid through the patch of curls at the juncture of her thighs, and then dipped lower, into her wet heat. His cock throbbed, and he groaned against her mouth.

Piper let out a gasp as his digits speared her. Her fingers dug tight into his shoulder, her nails creating little ellipses in his skin. Her breath came faster, and he felt as though his dick was going to burst from his jeans. It had been awhile, but he didn't want the embarrassment of creaming his pants just because he'd finally gotten his fingers inside her. She was so sexy, though, her cheeks flushed, those big, swollen breasts bouncing at the movement of his fingers pushing harder and faster into her tight channel. She'd been right when she said shifters even healed fast from childbirth. If he didn't know Theo was sleeping in the nursery, he'd never have known.

"I'm going to come," she gasped, her breath leaving her body in tiny moans. "Oh, God, Carter. Don't stop."

He had no intention of stopping, not as she unraveled around him, her head flung back, her back arched, pushing her tits into his face for him to feast on. His fingers were wet—dripping, in fact—and he knew he didn't need to worry about hurting her now as he took her.

"Oh, my God, Carter," she managed after she'd come back down. "You have no idea how long it's been since I had an orgasm."

He grinned down at her while he flicked the buckle of his belt open. The long ridge of his erection was clearly visible beneath the denim of his jeans. "Well, I hear they're like buses, 'cause two are about to come along at once."

She laughed and smacked her palm to her forehead. "Okay, stop talking now. You're almost too cheesy to have sex with."

He'd finished with his belt, and popped the button of his jeans and unzipped his fly. He pulled the jeans from his hips, letting them fall to the floor. His cock sprung out, thick and erect, pre-cum shining from the slit. He watched her gaze drop to his dick, her lips parting a fraction, her pink tongue flicking out across her lower lip.

"How about now?" he asked.

She reached for him. "I suddenly think I like buses."

They both grinned as he kneeled on the bed. He grabbed her ankles and yanked her down, pulling her so he slotted between her thighs. The scent of her—that same vanilla and cookies scent, but this time mixed with something muskier—made him almost lose his mind. He wanted to taste her, but he also wanted to fuck her, and it had been too long for him to wait any longer.

He kissed her again and reached between them, positioning himself at her entrance. She pushed her hips up to him, and he matched her movement, the head of his cock pressed against her entrance. She was so wet, and he eased inside her, still cautious about not wanting to hurt. Fuck, she felt good, though.

"It's okay," she said, her mouth against his ear, her tits pushing against his chest. "I'm not going to break."

That was all the encouragement he needed. He shunted forward, sliding the whole of his shaft deep inside her. They held still for a moment, letting her get used to his size, and his mind spun at the feel of her clamped around his cock. God, he could spend every moment for the rest of his life buried deep inside her, and he would die a happy man.

Her feet were around his hips, her heels digging into the hard muscle of his ass as he moved inside her. Their movements matched perfectly, their breathing ragged. One of his hands was knotted in her hair, the other was beneath her, his fingers dug into her ass cheek, yanking her up against him.

Piper cried out, and he felt her internal muscles tighten around him. Finally, he let himself go. His asshole, balls, right down his perineum, tightened and hot semen shot up through his cock. He pounded her so hard he thought they might both shatter. The noise he made wasn't human, and he didn't even care. He knew he was going to lose it. His orgasm was so powerful, he lost control of his movements and thoughts. He was giving himself to her in a way he'd never done with any woman before, coming hard inside her, and giving her a piece of his essence, his energy, his soul as he did so. He loved this woman, and he would give her every part of him, if he could.

Never had his wolf been so close to the surface while he'd remained in human form, and he could feel the urge to shift dangerously close. But then the orgasm faded, and the need to shift melted from him as well.

He lowered himself to one side and pulled Piper into his arms. They lay together, both chests heaving as they tried to catch their breath.

"That was incredible," she said.

He turned to kiss her, taking in the sight of her beautiful face, her pink, flushed cheeks, her perfect mouth. His chest contracted with emotion, and he knew he had to say the words. It had already been too long.

"You're so fucking amazing. I love you. I love every inch of you."

"I love you, too, Carter. I never thought I would be able to love a man, not after everything I went through, but you surprised me at every moment. You gave me faith in other people again. You gave me hope."

"I love you, Piper. You and Theo, too. It'll always be the three of us, okay? Nothing is ever going to take that away."

# Chapter Eighteen

"WILL YOU COME OUT INTO the forest with me?" Piper asked Carter one day as they were preparing breakfast. "It's been months since I last shifted, and now that I'm no longer pregnant, and Theo is getting bigger, my wolf is starting to get restless."

He grinned at her, that grin she had come to love. "I can't think of any way I'd rather spend the day. What about Theo, though?"

"I've already asked Anna if she'll watch him for a couple of hours, and she said she'd love to."

He caught her around the waist and planted a kiss on her mouth. "So that's a date, then."

She laughed. "Do you ever think that we did this all the wrong way around?"

"Yeah, but who gives a shit? I never much like conformity, anyway."

"Nah, me either."

The doorbell rang. It was Anna.

Theo was smiling now, and rewarded his new babysitter with a big, gummy grin.

"You sure you're going to be okay?" Piper asked.

"Absolutely. We're going to have a ton of fun, aren't we Theo?" Anna had slipped into baby-talk, just as most of them did when they were talking to the boy.

"Great. We'll be two hours, at the most. There's a bottle of expressed milk in the refrigerator, so it just needs to be put in hot water to warm it up, and his diapers and wipes are all in the change bag." She tried to think if she'd forgotten anything. "Oh, and you can find all his changes of clothes in the nursery."

The other woman flapped a hand. "I think I could have figured that one out for myself, Piper," she said, laughing. "Now go, before I change my mind."

"You're an angel. Thank you."

They left the house, hand in hand, and Carter dragged her over to his motorcycle. She climbed on the back, and he kicked it to life, the machine roaring beneath her. Piper felt like a completely different person than the one she'd been when Carter had first found her. That terrified young woman had nothing in common with the woman she was now. A mother. A mate. A viable member of the Silver Creek pack. She'd never believed she deserved such happiness.

Carter rode the bike the short distance to the edge of the forest, where he'd left his bike on the first day they'd met. They climbed off, and she grinned up excitedly at him. It was the first time they'd gone into the forest with something other than rescue on their minds.

"Now you're going to get naked, and I can't even have sex with you," he said reproachfully.

She gave a little shimmy as she peeled off her top. "I never said that was off the table, but you might have to catch me first."

"Now, that sounds like a challenge I can't refuse," he growled.

Piper threw her top to one side and got to work on her jeans, stopping to hop on one leg to pull them off, kicking her shoes off as well. Then she was moving again, ridding herself of her underwear as she went, knowing she was putting on a show for Carter and loving every minute of it.

As she threw her bra away, she finally allowed her wolf to rise to the surface. She sprang forward, and as her feet hit the ground, she'd morphed into the silver wolf that lived within her. From the growl behind her, she assumed Carter had also shifted, and she swung her head around to see the big, black wolf right on her tail. He darted forward and gave the backs of her legs a playful nip.

Then they were running, following scents and chasing rabbits. Two powerful animals, shoulder to shoulder, her noticeably smaller, but with him reducing his pace so they could run together.

Euphoria raced through her as the wind tore its fingers through her fur, and she ran with a freedom she'd never experienced before. She'd never been allowed to do this in her old life—just give in to her wilder side—and she loved every minute of it.

With their breath heaving, the two of them slowed to a trot.

Carter bumped up against her side, letting out a whine, and then nuzzled her mouth, licking at her nose, and she knew he was inhaling all the pheromones she gave off. He nipped at her fur, and Piper returned the gesture. She knew what he wanted, and slowed her pace again, coming to a standstill.

Carter moved up behind her and mounted her as a wolf, his front paws on her back, pressing her down with the weight of his body. He bit at the back of her neck, claiming her for his own.

The moment before he penetrated her, they both morphed back to human form, so the fur became the warm skin of his chest, which pressed against her smooth back. The sharp teeth became blunt as he bit the side of her neck, his erect cock pushing between her folds and spearing her. She took a gasp of breath in response to both the pain from him biting her, and the rough penetration, but quickly the pain morphed to pleasure. God, she didn't think she'd ever get bored of the feel of him inside her.

Still in animal mode, Carter growled above her as he thrust hard. There was something primal about them rutting on their hands and knees in the dirt, and she knew how this would be—rough, fast, satisfying. His arms wrapped around her, one across her breasts, his fingers clamping one of her nipples, and the other between her thighs to press on her clit. The feeling of him all over her sent her wild, and she gave voice to her pleasure, knowing they were in the middle of nowhere and only forest animals would hear her.

Her orgasm hit her hard and fast, making her toes curl in the dirt, and her fingers claw into the mud. Her inner muscles clamped down hard on Carter's cock, and he gave a primal grunt as he slammed into her, riding her climax. Then she felt his cock jerk, and heat pooled at her core as he emptied his cum deep inside her body.

They both fell still, breathing hard, Carter's sweaty chest still pressed against her back. He kissed the spot right behind her ear, sending a shiver through her. "We need to make this a regular thing," he said.

She smiled. "Absolutely."

He slipped from her body, and the hot spill of semen wetted her inner thighs. There was no point in cleaning up or even getting to her feet. They'd told Anna they'd only be a couple of hours, and Piper didn't want to be late on her first time away from Theo. She shifted to wolf, and beside her Carter did the same. They nuzzled each other, whining their affection, and then started to run back to where they'd left the bike.

BACK IN THE SPOT WHERE they'd abandoned their clothes, they both got dressed and climbed on the bike. Piper sat up close to Carter, pressing her face against the spot between his broad shoulder as they rode into town. She had a stupid grin on her face that she knew she wouldn't be able to wipe, even if she tried. She felt as though her happiness might cause her to explode, leaving only a bubbly little mess on the seat.

They reached town. On the street, one of the pack members waved down the bike, and Carter pulled over. Piper recognized the older man, but couldn't remember his name.

"Hey, Carter," the man said. "We've got a dispute going on about that house swap you signed off a few weeks ago. Seems one party has changed their minds, and the Farmer's aren't too happy about it. James is looking for you to try to sort it out. Can you stop by?"

"Sure. I'll just drop Piper home." He looked over his shoulder to her. "That's okay, isn't it?"

"Of course. Someone's got to get back for Theo." She climbed off. "But you go. I can walk from here."

"You sure?"

"Of course. It's only a couple of blocks."

He leaned in and kissed her. "I won't be long. Hopefully."

"Take your time."

Piper walked the couple of blocks home, still smiling privately to herself. She pushed open the front door and walked in.

"Hi, Anna," she called, "I'm back. Everything okay?"

No one answered, and she paused in the entrance hallway, frowning. Maybe Anna was upstairs, changing Theo. The house was big enough to not hear someone entering.

"Theo?" she called, even though it wasn't as if the baby could answer. "Anna?"

Something wasn't right; she could feel it in the air. If Theo was taking a nap, surely Anna would be down here. Maybe she was trying to get him to sleep, or she'd only just gotten him down, and didn't want to call back in case she woke him again. Though she was trying to reassure herself, Piper's heartrate had stepped up a notch.

She ran from room to room downstairs, double checking she hadn't missed anything, and then raced for the stairs. Using the banisters to haul herself up faster, she ran up the stairs, two by two.

"Anna? Theo?" Her voice came out frantic, and a cold fist of fear had clamped in the middle of her chest. She hadn't experienced this kind of fear for a long time, not since she'd made that fateful decision and run from her abusive husband. She wanted to believe Anna might have taken Theo on a walk, but she was sure Anna wouldn't have left the door unlocked without telling them, and the stroller had still been folded up in the hall.

Then it came, the thin wail of a baby. The sound a part of her had somehow both anticipated and dreaded all at the same time.

Adrenaline surged through her veins. "Theo!"

She pushed open the door to the room she now shared with Carter. Theo's crying immediately grew louder.

The first thing she saw was a crumpled form on the floor. "Anna!"

She stepped into the room. Had the other woman passed out? Or had there been an accident? Where was Theo? Had she been holding him when it happened?

Piper took a couple more steps, fully intending to check that Anna was okay, but something across the room made her freeze.

Horror crawled into her throat, her eyes widening, her breath locking in her chest.

Standing in the window was Finch Morgan. Her estranged husband.

And in his arms was Theo.

*Oh, God.*

A slow smile spread across her husband's face. Finch was almost twenty years older than she was, but he wore his age well. She hated how someone who looked so presentable hid such a dark core inside. He was the sort of man who could smooth talk anyone. The sort of man who would look at you as though you were crazy if you so much as suggested he was anything other than the attractive, charismatic man he portrayed.

"Hello, Piper. I thought I would introduce myself to my son, as it certainly seems as though you weren't intending to do so."

She broke her paralysis and took a step forward, her arms out. "Give him to me."

"I don't think so." He shifted the baby in his arms. Theo's cries grew louder, his face scrunching up into a red knot. The movement wasn't to make the baby more comfortable, but to expose something to Piper.

A knife pressed against his tiny side.

She snatched a breath. "No, Finch. Please. He's just a baby. He hasn't hurt anyone. It's me you need to blame."

"Oh, I do. Don't you worry about that. But I heard about the baby, and I started to think, 'what would be the best way to punish Piper for being so damned disobedient?' And I couldn't help but think that taking away the thing you'd been hiding from me all this time would be a pretty good place to start."

"He's not a thing," she managed to blurt. "He's a little baby. He's your son."

She hated admitting it out loud, but she'd have said anything at that point if it meant saving her son's life. She dared to cast a glance down at Anna. Was she still alive? The thought that Finch might have killed her made ice harden in her veins. She'd brought Finch into their lives. In a way, she was responsible, too.

"He *was* my son," Finch snarled. "But you've tainted him now, just like you tainted yourself. Don't think I don't know what you've been up to. You've had another man all over you—I can smell the stink of him from here—and you've allowed him to raise the baby."

"He's still your son," she insisted, praying if Finch could make an emotional connection to Theo, maybe he wouldn't hurt him.

"We'll see about that."

She didn't know what that meant.

"How did you find me?" she asked, trying to distract him from thoughts of wanting to kill Theo. The baby's cries had subsided into sad snuffles as he tried to push his little fist into his mouth, gumming it in desperation. The sight made Piper's heart ache. He was hungry, and she was desperate to feed him, but she knew Finch would never allow her to give her baby that comfort.

"That doesn't matter."

When would Carter be home? He'd said the thing he'd needed to deal with wouldn't take long, but how long had it been now? Twenty minutes since she'd climbed off the back of his bike and walked the rest of the way home, only to encounter her worst nightmare?

She put up her hands. "I'm sorry. I'll come back with you now. Both me and Theo."

He frowned. "Theo?" And then his features softened as he must have realized she was talking about the baby. "So that's what you called him."

"Yes, it's a good name. It suits him." She didn't want to have a conversation with him about her choice of names—she didn't want to have a conversation with him, period. But she was trying to buy time.

He gave his head a slight shake, as though throwing off whatever emotions or softening he might have experienced at hearing his child's name.

"I don't give a shit what his name is. He belongs to me now, just like you, and I'll do whatever the hell I want with both of you."

# Chapter Nineteen

CARTER PAUSED ON HIS porch. The front door stood slightly ajar, and though he couldn't quite pinpoint the reason, the sight made him uneasy.

He stepped inside, and his senses instantly went on high alert. There was a different scent in the house. One that was totally different from Piper, or the warm, milky scent of Theo. It wasn't even Anna. No, this was completely different. His sense of smell had always been particularly keen, and right now his nose told him this new person was male.

Though his first instinct was to call out to Piper, he bit down on the words, clamping them between gritted teeth and forcing himself to stay quiet. All the hairs on his arms rose to attention, and the muscles across his neck and shoulders tensed. He didn't know what was happening yet, but his body had gone into a fight or flight response. Deep inside him, his wolf growled a warning.

He moved slowly and as silently as his size would allow. The house should have been busy, with Piper and Anna most likely enjoying a coffee together—now that Piper was drinking coffee again—and Theo babbling or crying, but instead it was as though the house itself was holding its breath, and tension radiated through the walls. Something was wrong. Very wrong.

He followed his nose, which led him up the stairs, to the outside of their bedroom. The door stood slightly ajar.

Carter pressed himself closer, peering through the crack. In the window stood a strange man, and he was holding Theo. He was partially obscured by Piper standing with her back to him, and between them on the floor, Anna lay unconscious.

Immediately, he knew who this man was. Piper's husband.

Fuck. How did he find her? Someone must have told him. He'd never have stumbled across her by accident. Someone who wanted to hurt him and Piper. A couple of names sprang to mind, but now wasn't the time to start worrying about accusations. He needed to make sure Piper and Theo were all right.

"You're trespassing," he said, throwing open the door and stepping fully into the room. "Get the hell out of my house."

Piper half turned to him, one hand held out. "Carter, no!"

No? What did she mean no? Didn't she want him to help?

But then he caught a glimpse of silver in the sunlight, catching as it shone through the window directly behind the stranger. A knife. The man had a knife, and he was pressing it against Theo's rounded, defenseless tummy.

"Son of a bitch," Carter growled.

On the floor, Anna moaned and shifted slightly. At least she was still alive.

Piper looked terrified, and the sight made Carter want to kill the other man. But he couldn't do anything while the other man was holding a knife to Theo.

What kind of sick fuck threatened a helpless baby to get back at his wife?

"How are you planning for this to pan out?" Carter asked, his teeth gritted.

The other man gave a wolfish smile. He looked to be older than both of them, in his forties, at least. No wonder Piper had been so horrified having to marry him at the age of sixteen. He must have been twice her age back then. "Since you ask, I was planning on torturing Piper for awhile to make her understand how much pain and humiliation she put me through by running out on me like that. Now you're here, too, I can double the fun. Kill the baby to destroy Piper, and then kill Piper to destroy you."

Piper had been right when she'd told him this man was cruel. He was more than cruel. He was insane.

"Then you'll kill me, right?" Carter said, taking another step into the room.

"That sounds like a fitting ending to the story."

Carter squared his shoulders. "And you think I'm just going to allow that to happen?"

"Carter, please." Piper threw him a panicked look. He knew what the look said—that she didn't want him to push the son of a bitch and risk getting Theo hurt. But these kinds of men were ultimately cowards. They picked on young women and children because they were the ones he didn't expect to fight back.

He took another step.

Carter sought his memory to recall the man's name—Fitch, or was it Finch, he thought she'd said.

Whatever it was, the other man tensed, his jaw going rigid. "Don't take another step! I'll do it, I swear I will."

"Please, no!" Piper cried.

Theo had started to wail again, the breathy, hiccuppy cry of a child in distress. The sound was killing him, so he could only imagine how Piper must be feeling right now.

"It's okay. No one is going to do anything stupid."

Suddenly, in Finch's arms, the baby began to change. Theo's balled little fists became paws, and the broadening of his back caused the sleeper he wore to tear. From his flat little bottom, a curved tail appeared. His nose lengthened and turned black, creating a muzzle, and ears folded from the top of his head. Where previously there had been only pink gums, now Theo drew back his upper lip and snarled, revealing sharp little pup teeth.

And he put those teeth to good use.

With a ferocious snarl for something so small, he sank his little puppy teeth into the hand holding the knife. Finch gave a yell of shock and dropped what had been a baby only moments before, but was now a good-sized wolf-pup.

"Theo!" Piper yelled.

Carter saw his chance. Knowing he couldn't waste a single second, he threw himself forward. In midair, he shifted into wolf form. His front paws hit Finch directly in the chest, sending the man stumbling backward. One of the tall windows of the property was right behind him, and the force of a huge wolf shoving him back was enough to make him hit it.

Glass exploded outward, and with it went Finch. Carter caught a glimpse of fear and understanding in the man's eyes, his arms pinwheeling, before gravity took hold and he vanished out of view.

A second later, a massive crunch sounded from below as Finch hit the ground. From the street, someone screamed, "He's dead. Oh my God, he's dead!"

Piper ran to scoop up Theo, who'd shifted back to a baby again, pink and naked. Shifting took a huge amount of energy, and it was unusual for a baby of his age to manage it, and he wouldn't have been able to hold the shift for long. She picked him up and hugged him tight, half crying as she did.

"Oh, my baby. My beautiful, brave baby boy."

Knowing they'd have some serious explaining to do, Carter shifted back to man, and then went to his little family. He enveloped them both in his arms, feeling Piper shaking with emotion.

"Hush, it's going to be all right," he told them both. "He's gone. You're safe now. He'll never hurt either of you again."

"People are going to know now," Piper said, looking up at him, her tears matting her eyelashes. "They'll know the truth about who Theo's real father is."

He shook his head. "I don't care. All I care about is that both of you are safe. Nothing else matters to me."

And he held them both again until Piper's tears finally subsided.

# Chapter Twenty

PIPER WAS ON HER KNEES, wrapping china in tissue paper. Theo lay on a play-mat to one side, batting at the toys hanging down from a bar. He hadn't shifted again since the first time, and that was fine. It was easier to handle a baby than a wolf pup. They were packing stuff into boxes, planning to store away any family mementos Carter wanted to keep. His family had been in this house for generations, and there were things he said he wanted to take to their new place, wherever that may be.

They had to leave.

Nightmares of that day would haunt Piper's dreams for many nights to come.

Finch had died the moment he'd struck the ground, and though she knew he was dead, she also knew it would be a long time before she could ever truly shake the fear and anxiety caused from watching the man she hated most in the world hold a knife to her baby.

There had been no point in them trying to lie about the identity of the man who plummeted from Carter's bedroom window. More lies would only make things more complicated, and they needed to tell the truth in order for everyone to see that what had happened had purely been self-defense. Anna had also been there, and had made a full recovery after Finch had struck her across the head from behind as she'd been putting Theo down for a nap. She was able to testify about what had happened, and corroborate that both Piper and Carter were telling the truth.

They hoped there would be no backlash from Piper's old pack. Hopefully, they would be as pleased to be rid of Finch Morgan as she was.

Carter had been determined to find out how Finch had found them. Kimberly had been the first person he'd gone to, but she swore it hadn't been her. Then Liam had been the next suspect. In the end, his beta, James, had come forward, full of apologies. It seemed he'd had his eye on Carter's position after all, and when he'd suspected the baby wasn't Carter's, he'd done some research of his own, and figured out the rest for himself. Finch Morgan had put out feelers trying to find his estranged wife, and when James started asking around about missing female pack members, the two of them had put their heads together. James swore he hadn't expected things to end like this, and only wanted the truth to come out. He especially had never intended for Anna to get involved in any way. Carter had decided he couldn't come down too hard on him. After all, they had been the ones who had lied, and James hadn't known what a nasty son of a bitch Piper's husband had truly been.

Carter had told Piper he'd had no choice but to have James step down as beta. He didn't want to add more turmoil to his pack, especially as he now knew he was going to have to stand down as alpha. It put the pack in a position of great vulnerability to have neither an alpha nor beta at its head, though he told Piper he would stay in position until they found the right people to fill both spots.

A knock came at the door.

"I'll get it," Carter said, leaving the items he was wrapping.

But Piper was cautious now, even though she knew Finch was dead, and she got to her feet as well, following Carter to the door. She stood behind him as he opened it, peering out around the bulk of his frame.

To her surprise, half of the town appeared to be on their front porch, led by Liam and Kimberly, and Anna, and even James. She glimpsed numerous familiar faces.

"What is all this?" Carter said.

Liam led the way. "We need to talk to you about your position in the pack."

Piper reached out and touched Carter's forearm to offer him support. They'd known this day was coming.

Carter lifted his hands in submission. "It's okay, Liam. We're already packing. We can be out of here by tomorrow."

"That's not what I'm talking about."

He frowned. "You're not?"

"We've been doing some research, looking back on the rules of the pack. It seems there isn't anything anywhere in them that says an heir to the position of alpha needs to be biological. They say a son or a daughter, but there's no mention that the child can't be adopted."

Piper glanced up into Carter's face. A thrill of hope went through her at Liam's words, but Carter only frowned.

"What are you suggesting? That I legally adopt Theo?"

He nodded. "Yes, exactly. Legally adopt him, and he'll be seen as your son. As your heir. The boy is a shifter, he's already proven that, and as a pack, we can't see any reason for him to be seen as anything less than your and Piper's son."

Her heart swelled with hope, and she reached out and took Carter's hand. He still appeared pensive, his lips thinned.

"What about everything else? I lied to you all. Surely that has to be taken into consideration."

She wanted to kick him in the shin and tell him to shut the hell up, but this was Carter. He was alpha, and he wanted to do everything by the book.

Liam nodded. "We've talked about that. Considering the violent and dangerous man Piper used to be married to, we've decided it was understandable that you covered up her background, and the true parentage of Theo. You've always been a good alpha for this pack, Carter, and now you have a son—biological or not—there's no reason you can't continue to be our alpha."

Piper had to resist squealing and hopping up and down, clapping.

Carter still looked as though he couldn't quite believe what he was hearing. "So, I'm to adopt Theo?" He turned to Piper. "That needs to be your decision as much as mine."

Piper nodded and stood on tiptoes to kiss him on the cheek, the soft bristles of his stubble brushing her lips. "Of course I would want you to be Theo's legal father. You've been his dad ever since he was born. You delivered him, for goodness' sake. You've gotten up in the night with him, and changed his diapers, and paced the hallway with him when he wouldn't stop crying because he had colic. You are his dad, whether it's in blood or not."

For the first time since opening the door, a smile tugged at Carter's lips. He turned to her and pulled her to him and kissed her, right in front of half the town.

"Then that's what we'll do," he said. "And you'll be my alpha female, too."

Her heart swelled with happiness, an emotion only a few months earlier she'd never thought she'd get to experience. What more could she ask for?

Theo's mom.

Carter's mate.

A town she could finally call home.

THE END

LIKE WHAT YOU'VE READ? Sign up to Marissa Farrar's paranormal newsletter to learn about any giveaways, sales, or new releases! https://landing.mailerlite.com/webforms/landing/o0j7z7

# About the Author

MARISSA FARRAR HAS always been in love with being in love. But since she's been married for numerous years and has three young daughters, she's conducted her love affairs with multiple gorgeous men of the fictional persuasion.

The author of thirty novels, she has been a full time author for the last six years. She predominantly writes paranormal romance and urban fantasy, but has branched into contemporary fiction as well.

If you want to know more about Marissa, then please visit her website at www.marissa-farrar.blogspot.com. You can also find her at her facebook page, www.facebook.com/marissa.farrar.author or follow her on twitter @marissafarrar.

She loves to hear from readers and can be emailed at marissafarrar@hotmail.co.uk.

# Also by Marissa Farrar

**A Vampire Blood Courtesans Romance**
Stolen

**Bad Blood**
Shattered Hearts
Broken Minds
Tattered Souls

**Chronicles of the Four**
Through A Dragon's Eyes
With a Dragon's Heart
Into a Dragon's Soul

**Darkest Skies**
Their Invasion: Planet Athion
Her Resistance: Planet Athion

Our Uprising: Planet Athion
The Exodus: Planet Athion

## London Inked Boys
Carved in Ink
Bound by Ink
Forged with Ink

## The Dark Ridge Wolves
Wolf Snatched
Wolf Torn
Wolf Betrayed

## The Dhampyre Chronicles
Twisted Dreams
Twisted Magic

## The Mercenary Series
The Choice She Made
The Lie She Told
The Trust She Gave
The Trap She Faced

**The Monster Trilogy**
Defaced (A Dark Romance Novel)
Denied
Delivered
Caged Bird: The Monster Trilogy


**The Serenity Series**
Alone
Buried
Captured
Dominion
Endless
The Complete Serenity Series


**The Spirit Shifters**
Autumn's Blood
Saving Autumn
Autumn Rising
Autumn's War
Avenging Autumn
Autumn's End


**Standalone**
Underlife

The Sound of Crickets
Cut Too Deep
Of Blood & Moon
Survivor
No Second Chances
Three (An Alpha Male Boxed Set)
The Spirit Shifters: The Complete Series
The Monster Trilogy: The Complete Series
A Baby for the Alpha: Bad Alpha Dads
Fallen in Sin
The Dark Ridge Wolves: Books 1-3
Feathers, Fur, and Fantasy
London Inked Boys: The Complete Series
Chronicles of the Four
Dangerous Encounters: A Romantic Suspense Boxed Set
Darkest Skies: The Complete Series
Bad Blood: The Complete Series